JUST PLAIN MAGGIE

By LORRAINE BEIM

Illustrated by Barbara Cooney

A TAB BOOK

Published and distributed by TAB Books, Inc., an affiliate of
Scholastic Magazines, 33 West 42nd Street, New York 36, N. Y.

Other books by Lorraine Beim

BENJAMIN BUSYBODY
TRIUMPH CLEAR
SUGAR AND SPICE
ALICE'S FAMILY
HURRY BACK

Chapter One

Margaret Lowell shook herself like a dog and nudged open the back door. She was very careful to set her books down inside before she went in herself. Then she peeled off her raincoat and rubbers and left them out in the hall so she wouldn't track up the kitchen floor. When she closed the door behind her she no longer looked like a drowned rat but just like what she was. From her thick brown hair in pigtails, to her plaid cotton dress, to her white socks and loafers she was the picture of a twelve-year-old girl coming home from school.

"Mom," she called out. "Where are you?" She looked around for the cookie jar, took a handful and then went to the refrigerator for milk. Her motions were marked by frequent and annoyed glances at the window, the steady rain beating against it, spoiling all her plans for the afternoon.

She heard her mother coming downstairs then. "Oh, Mom," she wailed. "Now what will I do? Johnny and I were going fishing and now look. Hi," she remembered to greet her mother, and exchanged an affectionate hug. "I'm just furious. What can I do instead? What are you doing?"

"I've been up in the attic, doing chores. If you want to change your clothes and come up . . ."

A gleam of interest flashed across Maggie's face as she gulped down the last of her milk. "All right. Let's take out the old pictures." She ran upstairs and in a few minutes, in old blue jeans, joined her mother in the attic.

"Boy, listen to that." They heard the noisy patter of the heavy rain on the roof. "Wouldn't you know it would do this when we were going fishing? Maybe I can go in the morning?" she asked tentatively, knowing she usually helped around the house on Saturday morning.

Mother went on with the packing away of winter clothes, a jar of moth flakes in one hand. Maggie knelt before the old chest full of letters, papers, pictures, and odds and ends. She started rummaging and pulled out one of the old albums. Her mother's name was written across the front page. "Jane Nichols, Camp Woodlawn, Woodsville, New Hampshire." The first picture was of a big group of girls and women in middy blouses and something like gym bloomers. In the front row the smallest girls were holding a pennant that read CAMP WOODLAWN.

"Mom." Maggie looked up after studying the group. "Tell me about your camp."

2

Mrs. Lowell put her things down and came over to sit by her daughter. "My, I haven't seen those in a long time. Can you recognize me?" she asked.

Maggie found her mother readily and they both laughed over the clothes. "I look like you, don't I?" Maggie asked hopefully. It was true. Jane Nichols Lowell as a little girl had that same eager lively expression that Maggie had now. Neither of them would ever be called beautiful, but they looked like nice, interesting people.

They flipped through the pages showing Maggie's mother when she was fourteen with her bunk mates, with one or another of her friends, in a canoe, on a hike, dressed in costume, carrying a wastebasket and broom—all kinds of silly and funny pictures. Maggie asked, "Why don't I go to camp if it's so much fun?"

"Well, to tell you the truth," her mother answered, "Daddy and I were just talking about it the other night. We wondered if you would like to go and, though we'd miss you and be very lonesome by ourselves, we think it would be a good experience for you."

"You mean I can really go to camp, like on a vacation, and stay there?" Maggie asked, not quite believing her own ears.

"Yes, camps usually open right after school closes and end right before Labor Day. So you spend the whole summer there. Quite a vacation," her mother sighed.

That very night they talked it over with Daddy.

Daddy said, "It sounds pretty nice—a camp on a lake, with lots of girls to play with and counselors to take care of you and teach you swimming and tennis and riding and all the things girls do at camp . . ."

Maggie interrupted him. "Lots of girls?" That was

3

the phrase that stuck in her mind, that was important to her.

"Girls your own age too," Mommy added. "That's why we think it will be nice for you. You don't get much chance to meet other children, living way out here."

"But where do all the girls come from?" Maggie wanted to know. "What are they like?"

"They come from all over. Boston, New York, Philadelphia, and some from small towns and farms too. There are all kinds of nice girls."

The next day, Mother wrote to Camp Woodlawn but, to her disappointment, she found it was no longer in existence. So she sent for folders and catalogues of several camps that were highly recommended. Maggie pored over each one as they came. Some camps stressed the country atmosphere, some stressed work projects, they all had specialities of one kind or another. At Sunset Lake Camp it was water sports, and they appealed to Maggie. Mommy liked the sound of it for other reasons as well, so they wrote to ask if there was room for Maggie. The camp was limited to seventy girls, and its catalogue emphasized the fact that the counselors were all specially trained.

What excitement when the letter came accepting Maggie for that very summer! The director mailed them an application blank, a form for the family doctor to fill in about Maggie's health, and the list of what each girl needed. How Maggie concentrated on that list!

SUNSET LAKE CAMP

Camp colors are navy and cadet blue.
All clothes must be simple, washable, plainly marked and

4

in good repair. Following are the minimum requirements and some suggestions:

6 tee shirts, 3 of them white
2 regulation camp shirts, cadet blue
6 pairs shorts, 2 of them navy blue
6 pairs socks
2 pairs sturdy shoes
1 pair sneakers
6 sets underwear
4 pajamas
1 pair warm slacks
1 pair blue jeans
1 light sweater
1 heavy sweater
raincoat and rubbers
3 blankets
4 sheets
3 pillowcases
6 bath towels
3 washcloths
2 bathing suits
rubber poncho
1 flashlight and extra batteries
tennis racket and balls
toilet articles
writing materials including stamped envelopes addressed home
All articles must be plainly marked with washable name tapes.

Suggestions: Bring a few books, any musical instruments, camera with film, costumes, scarves, sewing kit, ribbons and such.

Laundry is sent out each week except for the first and the last week of camp.

We ask that you bring no expensive equipment or jewelry whose loss or damage would be of serious consequence.

Maggie knew that list by heart in a few days. She herself gave the mail carrier the letter ordering name tapes. Then they sent for the regulation shirts and shorts. Next she and Mother looked over Maggie's summer play clothes to see what she already had. Then they went on a couple of shopping sprees to buy the things she needed. When her equipment was complete they brought down from the attic the very trunk mother had used when she went to camp. After Daddy had given it a fresh coat of paint it looked like new. As a surprise Mr. Lowell painted M. L. on it with bright yellow paint which made Maggie feel very elegant.

Finally the trunk was ready to be closed and locked. Maggie and her mother had checked off everything on the list and added a few things besides. Maggie was so excited that she couldn't resist looking into the trunk again, to admire the neat orderly contents—her clothes, the bedding, her toilet articles and a few other precious possessions. But she was so keyed up she couldn't stay put for two minutes. She watched her mother sew name tapes on the last pair of socks, then she dashed over to look out the front window to see if Ann and Sally were coming up the road. Since they were not in sight she went over to her chest and picked up the five luggage tags. She got a lump in her throat every time she saw them, all neatly typewritten, one just like the other. In the corner in small letters they said: From A. S. Lowell, Pittsford, Mass. And then centered on each tag in capital letters they said:

TO MISS MARGARET LOWELL
SUNSET LAKE CAMP
LAKEVILLE, MAINE

Every time she read that—and she must have looked at those tags fifty times since Daddy brought them home last night—she would try to imagine herself there already. She would picture herself in her new camp shirts and shorts, walking along, arms linked with a whole crowd of girls. She thought of herself sitting in a big circle around a campfire, perhaps having a corn roast like the ones Mommy had told her about. And would she really be able to go swimming twice every day?

Maggie had never been away from her family before except to sleep over night at Sally's or Ann's house. She thought back now to that rainy afternoon when she had talked about going to a camp for the summer. She hadn't been able to believe it. It had seemed like talk, not something that would really happen to her.

When Maggie stopped to think about it she realized she had never known anyone who had been to camp except her mother and Johnny Elliot who had gone to Boy Scout camp for two weeks last summer. She remembered how envious she had felt of some of the things he did there, and now she herself was going for the whole summer.

Last week she had received a letter from the counselor and that had taken away the last doubt. Now she knew she was going, that it was real.

Dear Margaret [the letter had read],
   Welcome to our Sunset Lake family. I look forward to meeting you at camp next week. I am going to be your counselor in Bunk Five which we can all name together after we get to camp. I am sure you would like to know about the other girls in our bunk.
   Julie Burnett has her birthday right after we get to camp.

7

She will be twelve and she lives in Connecticut. Valerie Hunter is twelve already, her birthday was in March. She lives in New York City and this is her third year with us. Beth Morgan, who has been to camp for four years already but only came to Sunset Lake last year, was twelve in January and she lives right outside Washington, in Arlington, Virginia. Carol Tarrant comes all the way from Chicago and this will be her second year with us too.

So there will be five girls and your counselor in our bunk and I think we can look forward to a happy, healthy summer together. I come from Philadelphia and I teach science in a big school there. At camp I am your bunk counselor and I have charge of nature studies. I'll look for you so you can meet your bunk mates right away and waste no time in getting acquainted.

Until then, sincerely

Abbey Wittmer

This afternoon, in just a little while, Maggie's trunk would leave, and tomorrow afternoon she herself would leave and then she would meet Julie, Valerie, Beth and Carol for herself. She had read over Miss Wittmer's letter many times before it dawned on her she might be the only new girl in her bunk. Suppose she didn't know what to do? Suppose they didn't like her because she was new? She worried some about that but the anticipation of meeting four girls her own age helped. There weren't many girls in the village of Pittsford her own age. Ann Murray, who lived nearer the village than Maggie, was twelve too and they were good friends. Sally Solomon was fourteen but she played with Ann and Maggie a lot. Then there was Johnny Elliot who lived on the next farm and was in Maggie's grade at school. He was always around to go fishing with, or play ball or whatever they felt like.

But Ann, Sally and Maggie were the only girls between ten and fourteen who lived on this side of the village. They bicycled back and forth from school together.

Maggie was lost in thought when she heard Ann and Sally down in front.

"Maggie," they were both calling.

"Maggie . . ."

She fairly flew down the stairs to greet them. "My trunk is finished. It's ready to close. Daddy is going to take it down to the station for the four o'clock train. Want to go?" she asked.

The three of them jabbered away as though they hadn't seen one another for weeks instead of being at school for their report cards that morning.

"We brought you a present." Sally was grinning. "In case you decide to forget us here's a box of stationery."

"And here's a new fountain pen," Ann put in. "We expect you to write us a lot and tell us everything that happens."

"Oh!" Maggie was surprised and pleased. She hadn't expected anything like that. "Oh, Sally and Ann. I should give you presents," she laughed. And then when the package was unwrapped she saw the paper and envelopes were printed with her name and address in clear blue letters:

> Miss Margaret Lowell
> Sunset Lake Camp
> Lakeville, Maine

She let out a yell. "Mom!" She started up the stairs two at a time. "Come see what the girls have given me."

Mrs. Lowell was as tickled as Maggie to see the lovely present. "Why, girls, that was sweet and thoughtful of you. Maggie has no excuse for not writing often now, has she?"

Maggie had to laugh with the others. "I'll write every week, but you have to promise to answer. I'll be wanting to know what's going on here too." She tucked the box of paper into her trunk and put the fountain pen in the new purse Mom had gotten for her. "Gosh, how I wish you two were going with me."

Maggie sighed as she said it and she really meant it. She and Sally and Ann played together whenever they could. Sally lived near enough to bicycle back and forth often. Ann, who was the oldest of five children and had to be home a lot, joined them in her spare time. They always had lots of fun together and Maggie knew she would miss them.

The afternoon seemed to speed by. Daddy drove them all to the station to put the trunk on the four o'clock express train. They waved good-bye to it as though it were a friend. When they got back to Maggie's her mother had supper all ready for them and they made it last as long as they could. But all too soon it was time for Ann and Sally to go home.

Maggie thought she would never be able to get to sleep for all the things that were buzzing around in her head. The train trip, the girls' names, what camp looked like, swimming, leaving home and her friends, all these things whirled around in her mind so fast they finally put her to sleep.

"This is the day!" rang in her ears as she bounced out of bed next morning. She dressed carefully in the clothes Mommy had laid out for her, making sure she looked her best. After a careful examination of herself in the mirror she did her hair over again. She didn't want to make a bad impression. As she went down for breakfast she noticed it wasn't seven o'clock yet. How could she ever manage to wait for ten o'clock, when Daddy had said they would leave?

By the time she had finished her eggs, she wasn't in quite such a hurry. She sat dawdling over her milk and toast, not wanting to eat, not wanting breakfast to be over. Though camp and everything she knew about it sounded appealing, the thought that she wouldn't see Mommy and Daddy for over a month was very scary. Visitors were received at camp only the first week end in August, so she would have a long wait. As the clock ticked on, she trailed her mother around like a puppy dog.

When Mrs. Lowell went up to get dressed Maggie almost burst into tears. "Will you write me every day?" she asked, a catch in her voice.

Mommy put her arms around Maggie. "You bet I will. And just remember that we'll miss you every minute you are away, having a wonderful time up in Maine with all those girls. Be sure to write us too. Don't forget us while you are so busy having fun, will you, Maggie?"

Maggie loved her mother for talking that way. Though her hands were clammy at the thought of saying good-bye she began to think about camp again and all the good times she would have.

"Let's get all set, Maggie," her daddy called. "Where's your purse?"

She had it right over her shoulder. "Here," she answered.

"O.K., now let's see. What have you in there already?"

"Here's my hankie, and the fountain pen that Ann gave me, and here's my money—let's see, sixty-eight cents. And here's a comb, and a postal addressed to you so I can mail it as soon as I get there. And here's the tag I'm supposed to wear around my neck the first few days. The camp booklet says all the girls wear them. Where's my ticket?"

"Right here." Daddy took out his wallet. "Put it away carefully. And give it to the conductor on the train. He will give you back the part you need from Boston on. And the return trip too. And here's some more money for your change purse." Daddy counted out five new crisp dollar bills. "You may want something on the train. You don't have to spend it but if you need it you have it." Daddy gave her a big hug after she put the money away. "And have a scrumptious time, Magpie, because we'll miss your smiling face around here and if you aren't having lots of fun —why, we'd rather have you home with us."

Maggie couldn't hold the tears back now. "Oh, Daddy," she sobbed on his shoulder. "I want to go so much and I want to stay here with you and Mom."

"Well, that's nice to hear." He cupped her chin in his hand. "You know, Maggie, I'd feel pretty badly if you weren't just a little bit sorry to leave us. But Mother and I are willing to be lonesome so that you can have new experiences and meet lots of girls and enjoy yourself. And we can hardly wait for visitors day so we can come to see you."

Mommy held Maggie's overnight case and her own hat and gloves as she came into the living room. "All ready," she said. "We can get started now."

"Good-bye, Sammy." Maggie patted her dog. "Here, Parsnip," she called to the cat. "Be good while I'm away. I'll miss you." She kept looking back at the house as they drove off down the road, into the village and to the station.

Maggie carried her own suitcase when she got out of the car. She had her hands full now—besides her suitcase she had her purse, her raincoat and her new tennis racket in its press. She was so busy trying to get it all under control that she didn't see Johnny Elliot waiting there for her.

"Hi, Maggie." He sauntered up. "Here's something for you on the train."

"Why, Johnny. Gee, thanks!" She freed two fingers to take the paper bag he held out to her. "Chocolate and bubble gum. Oh, that's swell. Thanks again."

"Yeah, have a good summer. You'll like it, I know. I'm going to Scout camp the end of July. If you have half as much fun as we do, it will be good."

"Oh, sure." She kept looking down the track, impatient for the train now, eager to get this over with and be on her way. "We'll get together when I come home and compare notes. You have a good time too."

"Don't forget to send us the postcard in your excitement," Daddy cautioned.

"Here she comes!" Mommy heard the train first. Both Mommy and Daddy climbed on the train for a moment to see that Maggie got settled with all her belongings. Then Maggie watched them standing on the platform outside, waving good-bye till she couldn't see them any more.

The whole trip was a blur—fields, towns, trees, cows, horses, scenery framed by the windows of a train—until she met the camp train at Portland.

Miss Wittmer was waiting for Maggie when she got out of her train, and she took her right into the camp train. She led her from one end of the coach to the other, finding and then introducing her to her bunk mates. Maggie was so taken aback by the cheering and yelling of the girls that she hardly knew what was happening. Every seat in the car was crowded with girls, talking, laughing, paying no mind to what was going on around them. Miss Wittmer had to yell to get their attention. By the time Maggie was settled in a seat opposite Carol Tarrant and Julie Burnett, it was almost time to get off the train.

Maggie piled into one of the big busses waiting to take them all to camp. She felt almost breathless with excitement as she squeezed into a seat and the bus lumbered off. After a short ride, while the dusk deepened into night, the girls began cheering again.

"At last!"

"We're here!"

Maggie peered out of the bus just in time to catch the headlights picking up the big sign over the side road that read, "SUNSET LAKE CAMP."

Chapter Two

"I'M HERE BECAUSE I'M HERE BECAUSE I'M HERE BECAUSE I'm here . . ." A voice next to Maggie woke her with a start. Then she heard the silvery tones of a bugle filling the crisp morning air. She sat up, her legs crossed under her, looking with sleepy eyes at each bed. The sun was pouring through the door, filling the bunk with brightness. Her first day in camp!

Last night she must have fallen asleep as soon as her head touched the pillow. The excitement of being on the camp train, of meeting her bunk mates was all she could remember. The arrival at camp was only a blurred memory. As she looked about now, trying to get used to what she saw, one head after another popped up. It was Carol who was singing in tune with the bugle, she saw. There was Beth right across from her, and Julie on the other side. Just then the bathroom door opened and Valerie came out. By the time the bugle had finished blowing reveille, Miss Wittmer's head came up too.

Maggie's eyes were big, taking in everything. She remembered vaguely how bare the bunk had looked last night when they arrived—six empty beds, three against each long wall. There was a door at either end, one leading outside and one leading to the bathroom. Four trunks were standing in the middle of the room, and there were some empty shelves and hooks on either side of both doors. The side walls were just a little higher than the beds. Above that the walls were made of screening with canvas sides to roll down when it rained.

Some of the girls started to get up, but Maggie stayed right in her bed. "Hi," she said almost under her breath. "Why, I know all your names already . . ."

"Hi" and "Good morning" and "Welcome" and "C'mon" were some of the greetings she got in return.

"Abbey, what'll I wear? My trunk hasn't come yet," she heard Julie ask. Abbey! So you called the counselor by her first name. Maggie's trunk hadn't arrived yet either and she didn't know what to do. She would wait and see.

Valerie threw a pair of shorts and a shirt at Julie and another pair at Maggie. "Here, you two, wear these till your trunks get here." Then Valerie looked at Maggie intently. "If the shorts are too wide I have a pin. Say, do you have a nickname or do they call you Margaret? I'm Val for short."

"I'm Maggie. When anyone calls me Margaret I look to see who they're talking to. Even in school my teacher calls me Maggie." She was putting on the shorts now. "I guess I'll need that pin, Val. And thanks a lot, I didn't know what to do."

"Maggie for Margaret," Beth snorted from across the bunk. "How can you stand that? We'll call you Peggy, that's a nickname for Margaret too."

"No, I don't think so," Maggie answered. "I've always been called Maggie. I'm sort of used to it."

"But it's so ordinary, like a washlady with a knot on top of her head." Beth was laughing at her. "I don't like it."

"You're crazy," Carol spoke up. "I like Maggie, it's a friendly, unstuck-up kind of name."

"Better get going," Abbey called. The girls got busy brushing teeth, combing hair and hurrying for breakfast.

"C'mon, Maggie," Carol told her. "We do setups before breakfast. After swimming tests you can have a duck in the lake instead, if you want, but at first everybody does setups."

"Mmm." Maggie felt relieved to hear about swimming before breakfast. Why doesn't Beth like my name, she thought. Maybe it isn't fancy enough for her. "Well, Maggie's my nickname whether Beth likes it or not," she said out loud as she and Carol walked along.

"Beth is a funny duck, don't pay too much attention to what she says. Last summer I used to fight with her all the time. I hated being in the same bunk with her, because she's always picking on someone. When I heard she was in our bunk again I didn't feel so much like coming. But you get used to her. And wait till you see her swim and play tennis and all. There isn't anything that girl can't do. She's a whizz at everything. She plays the piano and sings and dances too. I have to say that for her."

17

"Gosh, I hope you don't mind having me in your bunk," Maggie answered. "I've never been to camp before. But I do know how to swim."

"It's funny about Beth," Carol went on. "Because she is so good at everything, she thinks the rest of us should do whatever she wants. She's too bossy—but when you see her in action you can't help admiring her."

Maggie was listening but she was also getting her first good look at camp. Last night she hadn't been able to see what the place looked like. The mist was rising from the lake now in the early morning sunshine and it looked inviting. She could see a nice sandy-looking shore line and all around her were the woods in which the bunks nestled. They were not in a straight line but were set here and there among the trees. She counted them—five in all—and there was the main house as well. It had a big screened dining porch overlooking the lake. Then she noticed there were more bunks on the other side.

"How many bunks are there all together?" Maggie asked.

"Nine others like ours," Carol told her. "That makes ten. Miss Strang has her own bunk with the infirmary in it. She's the nurse, you know. There it is over by the Ranch."

They were in back of the main house now, in a large open space. The Ranch, which Maggie knew from the catalogue was the recreation hall where they had dances and movies and shows, was up on a knoll opposite the main house. She saw the infirmary and she also saw the whole camp assembling in the clearing for

This was the road they had driven in on last night, setups.

she realized. Her eyes followed the road till Carol told her, "The tennis courts and the ball fields are out there a ways. We passed them coming into camp." Maggie was taking it all in as Carol went on talking. "Isn't this a beautiful place? The lake is super. It's almost a mile wide and about five miles long. You'll see it all later."

After setting-up exercises they went in to breakfast, where every bunk had its own table. Miss Wright, who was camp director, said good morning to each girl. Maggie counted eleven tables but only ten of them had campers. Miss Wright's table was a big one and the nurse, the head counselor, and the head of all water sports sat with her.

They had oranges and all the pancakes and cocoa they could stuff into themselves. When they had finished Miss Wright got up to speak. "Today is settling day. Go back to your bunks and arrange them to suit yourselves as long as they're neat. Some of your trunks haven't arrived yet but I'm sure the other girls will help you out. At eleven we'll blow the whistle for swimming. Miss Brown will tell you about that."

"Yea, Brownie!" Everybody cheered and clapped as Miss Brown got up. Maggie could see the girls were crazy about her.

"It feels awfully good to be back here with you," she started. "And I know we're going to have a prize lot of swimmers this summer. But until we have a chance to give tests these are the rules. White caps are advanced swimmers. All last year's white caps may use the diving board, the big float and the water in between. But they may not go beyond that until they take their tests again. Green caps are the intermediate swimmers. All green caps, until they pass their tests again this year, can go only to the end of the pier and as far out as the rowboats where Miss Paul and Miss Marion will be on duty. All new campers and red caps —red caps are the beginning swimmers—must stay in the crib. Is that clear?"

The girls nodded in agreement and Brownie went on. "For the benefit of the new campers and to remind the old ones, no one goes in the water till the signal is given. Only Paulie or I give that signal. It is a double blast on the whistle. And whenever you hear a whistle blow three times it means swimming is over and you come right out of the water. We don't fool with these signals and these rules. Anyone who can't follow them has to stay out of the water until she shows she knows what they mean. There is no second chance on water rules."

"When will you start giving tests?" Beth asked, right from Maggie's table.

"This afternoon we'll start with Miss Todd's senior Bunk One. I think we might take Bunk Two also, don't you, Paulie?"

"Yes, oh, yes!" The girls from Bunk Two were jumping up and down. "Take us too," they chimed in.

"We'll get to all of you in a few days. I'll be seeing you at the water." Brownie sat down, and the girls got up to leave the dining room.

Maggie watched to see what the other girls did and then followed them. She walked along toward her bunk behind Carol, Val and Abbey Wittmer who were all chatting away in front of her. But Maggie was lost in a world of her own. She was such a stranger here and there was so much she didn't know. Bugles, two whistles, three whistles, red caps or white caps, girls' names, the way of doing things. Had Mommy's camp been like this, she wondered. Thinking of her mother, Maggie felt a great wave of homesickness, a need to see something, be with someone she knew. She couldn't go into the bunk with the other girls. She was afraid if anyone said one word to her she would cry and she didn't want to do that.

So she walked down toward the lake by herself. She stood by the shore, looking over the glistening water, trying to swallow the great lump in her throat. She wasn't home, she was at camp because she had wanted to come. She would get used to it—to the girls and the way of doing things. She guessed it would be all right. But she did miss home and all the familiar places and people.

In a few minutes she hurried back to the bunk to see what was going on, and to find out what she should do next. As she went in she realized that no one had noticed she hadn't been around all the time. It didn't matter, apparently, whether she was there or not. "How can I find out about my trunk?" she asked her counselor.

"They'll bring it to the bunk when it arrives," Abbey told her. "Do you need anything?"

"I have no bathing suit. . . ."

"You can wear one of mine," Val told her.

"Are you sure you can spare it? I'd hate to miss a swim."

"Val has everything," Carol put in. "Whenever you need something, no matter what it is, Val has it. Just take a look at her trunk sometime. You should see her costumes—cowboys, or old-fashioned girls or ballet stuff."

"This year I have an evening dress," Val laughed.

"Pink taffeta with a great big wired skirt. I got it for my birthday party."

"Lucky you!" Carol's eyes were popping. "I'd never get anything like that. An evening dress! Jeepers! Show it to us . . ."

"Oh!"

"How gorgeous!" The girls were breathless as Val took it out of her trunk. "How stunning!"

"Gee, they let you bring it to camp," Beth said in amazement.

"Yes, I convinced them we could use it as a fancy dress costume or for a play. And we probably will," Val laughed.

"She looked beautiful in it," Julie told them. "I was at her party and it was—well, just like in the movies. The best time ever. I wish I didn't have a camp birthday."

"Me too," Carol added. "But it wouldn't do me any good if I had my birthday at home. I'd never get a dress like that. My party dress is like any other dress only it's silk. My mother wouldn't even let me have boys over for New Year's Eve. I just had a school friend spend the night. My brothers were both out."

"Do you go out with boys?" Julie asked Maggie as they were making their beds.

"Go out?" Even the question was puzzling to Maggie. She played with Johnny Elliot, they went fishing together and things like that. But going out, just what did she mean? "Well, I have a friend who is a boy," she answered. "But it's different where I live. You couldn't go out, there's no place to go."

"Well, does he come to your house at night and do you dance and stuff like that?" Julie wanted to know.

"Johnny doesn't know how to dance. Sometimes we

fish for a little while after supper. Is that what you mean?" Maggie and Julie were whispering quietly so the others wouldn't hear.

"No, I mean dates and things. I don't go out either. Except when I went to Val's for the week end. She had a big birthday party with boys and music, and the next day we went horseback riding in Central Park with two boys. We all went back to her house for lunch and then we fooled around. But home is different. I know some boys from school but we never go out or anything like that."

The conversation from across the room drifted over to them now. ". . . at least this year I'm allowed to go off with the other girls for lunch by myself on Saturday. We go every week, four of us, and then to the show. Boy, we saw *Little Women* a couple of weeks ago and I cried buckets full."

"Oh, I saw that in Washington," Beth spoke up. "It was pretty good. But I like Westerns better than that love stuff. Have you seen *The Texans* on television Friday nights? I like television better than the movies cause there's more to see. I hear there's a television set at camp."

"There is!" Abbey told them. "You can see the aerial on top of the Ranch." As she noticed the looks on the girls' faces she went on, "But it is only to be used by permission and then only for special programs. So don't get any ideas about parking there."

Maggie listened hard to this conversation buzzing around her but she could take no part in it. She didn't have anything to say. What did she do on Saturdays? She might play with Sally or Ann or Johnny, she might help to clean the house and maybe bake something. In the afternoon she usually went to town in the car with Mommy and Daddy while they shopped, and sometimes they took her to a movie. She had never been to a restaurant alone with other kids—unless going to the drugstore during lunch period for ice cream counted.

"What do you want, Bobbie?" Maggie looked up to see to whom Julie was talking. It was a little girl, about nine or ten.

"I have nothing to wear," Bobbie lamented. "When will the trunks come? What shall I do?"

Maggie's heart went out to her—she knew just how she felt.

"Isn't there someone in your bunk who can lend you some shorts till the trunks come? I told Mother she ought to send the trunks off a day earlier. But no, that was her day in town."

"Hi, Val!" Bobbie was looking around. "Mary and I are the only old girls in our bunk. And one of the new girls is crying her eyes out. She wants to go home."

"Barbara Burnett," Abbey greeted her. And then Maggie knew she was Julie's sister. "How are you? Do you remember how you cried last year at this time? But you're so much bigger now I guess you forget how it feels to be the camp baby."

Bobbie looked sheepish. "None of the new kids know what to do. Even our counselor is new. We have the one who is going to do the shows. Her name is Mickey Fisher. She looks like an actress to me."

"Skat, pest," Julie said to her. "Did you mail your postal to Mother?"

"Yes, I did. So there!" Bobbie felt very grown-up about that. "But how's Daddy going to know we're here?" she wanted to know.

"I'm writing him today," Julie answered. Maggie

24

looked bewildered. Wouldn't Julie's daddy just naturally know, wouldn't her mother be sure to tell him? "Is he away on a trip?" she asked.

"No," Julie answered in a strange, flat tone of voice. "My father lives in New York and we live in Connecticut with my mother."

"How can that be?" The words slipped out of Maggie's mouth before she had a chance to think.

"They're divorced, dopey," Beth told her. "Are you such a hick that you never heard of it?"

Maggie could have bitten her tongue off for asking. She felt so bad that she couldn't help blurting out, "I'm sorry, Julie. Please excuse me." She felt the color mounting in her face, and she wished she could run away. She couldn't look at the other girls. Maybe she was a hick, but she just didn't know anyone that was divorced. How would she ever be able to look at Julie again? Julie's mother and father living in different places! When did she see her father? That must be awful.

"Julie, why don't you take Bobbie back to her bunk and see if you can help out?" Abbey suggested. Maggie watched as Julie walked her sister back, but she felt speechless and dumb and her eyes filled with tears.

"Hey, kids," Carol spoke up. "What kind of a party are we going to give Julie? Tomorrow is her birthday. Let's plan something good . . ."

"A steak roast at the point!" Val suggested.

"No, a square dance would be better." Beth spoke now. "We'll invite the whole camp and that would be more fun."

"Julie has a better time with just a few people," Val insisted. "I know she would like a steak roast. Just our bunk and maybe Bobbie, and we could ask Brownie and Miss Wright. A real surprise party too. You can all go there and get ready and I'll bring her down about five o'clock. When Brownie comes she can bring the ice cream." Val had it all planned, and before long everyone but Beth agreed with her.

"Well, then we'll come back and square dance after," Beth kept on.

"The fun of a steak roast is sitting around the camp fire after it, singing and talking," Carol argued. "Anyway we'll probably square dance Saturday night."

Maggie only listened to the discussion. She felt quite out of it, because she didn't know enough about camp to help with the plans. The one time she had joined in the conversation she had put her foot in it, asking Julie to explain about her parents.

She walked over to Abbey. "I feel so bad," she told her. "I didn't know about Julie's family. I shouldn't have said anything. What can I do about it?"

"It's no secret, Maggie," Abbey told her. "And there's nothing for you to do about it. All the other girls knew it. Julie's mother and father were divorced over a year ago. Julie isn't happy about it, naturally, but that can't be helped and you needn't worry."

Just then the station wagon drew up with Maggie's and Julie's trunks on it. It made Maggie feel happier to see something of her own, something she knew, her shining trunk with M. L. printed on it in big letters. She got her key from her purse and as soon as she had it open and her own things out she returned what she had borrowed from Val. "Thanks, thanks a lot," she said to her.

"Any time." Val went right on writing a letter.

Maggie decided she would write a letter too. But she wouldn't let on that she was homesick. She would tell about camp, and how they were going to celebrate one of the girl's birthdays. She didn't want Mommy and Daddy to worry about her.

After she had written a letter to Mommy and Daddy, she wrote to Ann and Sally too. She missed them a lot, and she was almost certain she would never be able to like the girls in her bunk as much as either Ann or Sally.

When Maggie had finished her letters, she looked up to see what the other girls were doing. Beth was re-arranging her clothes.

"Look at my new bathing suit," Beth said, holding up a snowy white bra and shorts with a little bit of blue trim just the color of her eyes. Maggie had never known anyone with a suit like that. "Gee," she said. "It's beautiful!" She was sure it would look wonderful on Beth. Even though Beth did act superior, Maggie had to admit she was pretty.

"Pretty fancy, isn't it?" Carol was needling Beth again.

Maggie thought of her own bathing suits. They were nice, and she had been delighted when Mommy bought them. But they could look plain next to the shining white of Beth's. That was the way Maggie felt too. These girls were all so different, so strange to her. They knew things she didn't know anything about. Divorced parents, evening clothes, dates with boys, all kinds of things. What would they think of her?

She had never been to the kinds of places they talked about, she had never done all the things they took for granted. Sally and Ann were not at all like these girls. Would she ever be able to make friends here? The girls in camp looked nice, and they were all between ten and fifteen years old, but that seemed to be the only way in which they were at all familiar. Maggie felt lonely; it seemed as though there was nothing she could say to these girls. What could she tell them about herself? That she went to Pittsford Central School, that she had some good friends and they played together, went fishing, listened to the radio? Or that she had had her tonsils out at the hospital in Springfield when she was eight?

If the whistle hadn't blown for swimming just then, Maggie would surely have burst into tears.

Chapter Three

A FEW DAYS LATER MAGGIE WAS STANDING FIFTH IN LINE on the pier waiting to take her first swimming test. She was proud of the fact that she already knew how to swim. She had wanted to be able to go fishing in a boat, but Daddy had said she could go in a boat only when she knew how to swim. She remembered now how hard she had tried to learn a few summers ago. It hadn't taken her long. She could swim in deep water, she wasn't afraid to get her face wet, and she could jump in feet first. So the swimming test didn't worry her at all.

As she came next to the head of the line, she watched the girl taking the test closely to see what she would have to do. First the girl dove off the end of the pier. That looked easy. Then she had to swim half way out to the float, circle the rowboat that was bobbing up and down, and swim back to the pier again. Tread water! What was that? Maggie watched carefully and saw the girl in the water pumping with her feet, keeping her hands up close to her head, out of the water. Maggie giggled to herself. It looked like such fun she could hardly wait to try it.

"Next!" Brownie's voice sang out.

"I'm Margaret Lowell." Her voice came out in a husky whisper. But she gulped and went on. "Maggie for short. Bunk Five. I'd like to try the intermediate test."

"Fine," Brownie said and then told her, "Dive in head first, then swim out to Paulie's rowboat, swim all around it, turn and swim back. When you get back you can float for a minute and then tread water. Are you ready?"

Maggie's heart was pumping like a steam engine. She had never gone into the water head first but she didn't hesitate. She leaned over from her waist, head lower and lower, until she actually fell into the water. "I did it! I did it!" The words chimed in her head as she pushed her way to the surface again. She rubbed the water out of her eyes and looked up at Brownie.

"Good try," Brownie called to her. "Now make for the boat."

Maggie set out, thrashing through the water as fast as she could go. The boat didn't seem to get much nearer as her arms waved and her legs kicked and she puffed to get her breath. She didn't swim with her head in the water as she saw some of the girls do, but she worked just as hard. A little bit more and she would be at the boat.

"Take it easy," Paulie was talking to her in a quiet

voice. "This is only to see if you can swim, this is not a race."

"A race?" Maggie shouted back at her, and looked around to see who was racing with her.

"No." Paulie leaned over the edge of the boat, smiling at her. "Take it easy. You don't have to race. If you work so hard you'll be all tired out before you get through. You're doing fine. Now go back nice and easy."

Maggie was tired by the time she got back to the pier. She was glad to stretch out on her back for a minute and float. Her chest rose and fell with her heavy breathing. But she was floating, she could see that as she took a peak at her toes sticking up out of the water. She simply had to pass the test. She didn't want to stay with the beginners, and Brownie wouldn't let her go in a boat till she could wear a green cap. Her thoughts were interrupted by a poke in the tummy.

With a start Maggie looked up. "That's it," Brownie was yelling at her and laughing. "Did you fall asleep?" Maggie was treading water already. Her hands out of the water and close to her head, she kept pumping with her feet. It felt like riding a bicycle uphill. She kept watching Brownie who looked from Maggie to her watch. In what seemed like no time at all Brownie motioned to her to come out of the water.

"You're a fish," Brownie told her. "With a green cap." A smile spread across Maggie's face. She could hardly believe her ears as Brownie went on talking to her. "Now you can go out to the float during swimming periods. The counselor on duty there will help you with your strokes. I wouldn't be surprised if before too long you will be coming to take your white cap test. Practice on it and I'll keep an eye on you. You can also go in the rowboats," Brownie called after her as Maggie went racing back to her bunk.

"I passed! I got a green cap. And maybe I'll get a white cap!" She was practically bursting with the news. She was disappointed to find only Beth in the bunk.

"Don't count your chickens," Beth answered. "I was the only one in the group last year who got a white cap. You have to be awfully good to get it, so don't be too sure of yourself."

"Well, Brownie said so," Maggie told her, feeling quite confident. "What do you have to do?"

"You have to know two strokes in good form, swim a quarter of a mile, undress in the water, climb in and out of a canoe without upsetting it, fetch a plate from ten feet of water on a surface dive. Oh, and lots more, so don't get your hopes up. I saw you swim yesterday and all you know is the dog paddle. You can keep yourself afloat, but you don't even know how to do the breast stroke."

Abbey came into the bunk just then and Beth said no more. But Maggie, who had been so proud of herself and so elated just a few moments ago, stood by her bed feeling lost and forlorn again. Beth had certainly taken away the only joy she had felt here at camp.

"What's the matter?" Abbey asked her. "Didn't you pass your test?"

"Yes." Maggie's face brightened. "I got a green cap and Brownie told me to practice up and try for a white cap."

"Then smile, girl!" Abbey was pleased. Maggie could see that. "That's just fine," Abbey went on. "We'll all help you. Go to Fran during swimming period and Paulie in the afternoon and see how quickly you can do it."

"Oh, I will. And now I want to write home and tell them about it. Daddy will be so glad." She went for her pen and paper. "He taught me how to swim."

"I'm a green cap," Carol came dancing into the bunk. "Hurray for me. Last year it took me over three weeks to get it. This year right away, first try. Hurray! Hurray!" She threw the cap up into the air. "Abbey, do you think I'll be allowed to make an overnight trip? Oh, I hope, I hope . . ."

Those words intrigued Maggie, though she didn't quite understand what Carol meant. An overnight trip? If she got a green cap? But it must be good because Carol wanted to go so much. Go where? "Where do you go on an overnight trip?" she asked.

"I don't go—at least I didn't last year. I can't get my head under water because I have bad sinus, so I'm not allowed to dive. But those who can go different places. One trip is up the lake, over the portage to the Penobscot River. Or they go down the lake through another portage and over to Big Rockwood Lake. They pack the canoes with food and blanket packs and stay out overnight. Out of camp two whole days! It's like the steak roast we had for Julie only it starts right after breakfast one day and you don't come back till suppertime the next. And when you're a senior and a white cap there are longer trips. Last year the senior trip was all the way up the Penobscot River to the Millinocket Lakes, through three portages and a few small carries, and they were gone for four nights. I'm coming to camp until I can make the big trip. Then I'll feel I've really lived. The trips are the best part of camp, don't you think so, Abbey?"

While Carol and Abbey went on talking, Maggie listened with one ear and began her letter home.

33

Darlings, I got a green cap today. I can swim. I can go out on the float now and the head lady, her name is Brownie, said I should work for a white cap. So I will. The girls say we may take an overnight trip in the boats. I would like that. A couple of nights ago we had a party for Julie who was twelve years old. Just our bunk and her sister and the two heads, Brownie and Alice Wright. We went to a place near camp by the lake where there is an outdoor stove and we cooked steak and ate tomatoes and potato sticks and carrots and had ice cream and cake for the party. This camp makes beautiful cakes for birthdays with your name on it in any color and candles and it was very nice. Carol has her birthday in August. Then we sat by the fire and they sang a lot of camp songs that I didn't know and then lots of songs I did know from the radio and school. Miss you so very very much. Even more than that. When I'm not swimming I keep wishing I was home. I hope the time for you to come see me gets here very quick. I'm going to write the girls so you be sure they answer me. I want to get a lot of letters.

Love and kisses

Maggie

That was a pretty long letter and when it was finished Maggie went to the main house to mail it. She felt more like mailing herself home and leaving the letter in camp. Since it was suppertime she stayed at the main house, and after they had finished eating, Julie's sister asked Maggie if she would help her to write a letter.

"I have things to say I don't want my counselor to know and I need help. You seem so nice I thought you would help me." Bobbie looked up to Maggie with such hopeful pleading that she couldn't possibly refuse. Someone had noticed Maggie, someone needed her, asked her to help, if it was only to write a letter.

"Sure thing," Maggie assured her. But then she wondered why Bobbie didn't ask Julie to help her. They

34

walked up to Bobbie's bunk together. It was the first time Maggie had been in another of the bunks. It was just like hers only the girls were younger and there was a little more mess.

"I don't want to say in here," Bobbie whispered as they went in. "I don't want the kids to know about this. Let's go out."

They finally settled down on a big rock under the trees and Bobbie started her letter.

Daddy dear, Please come up on ("How do you spell *parents?*" she asked Maggie.) Even if Mother doesn't want you to it is my ("How do you spell *visitors?*") visitors week end and I want you both to be here with me. I need you and you'd better come. If you don't come I won't stay in this camp. I'll run away and you'll never see me again. Love Barbara.

"Do you think your father will like that letter?" Maggie asked her. "Suppose he can't come then. Think how bad he will feel."

"He can come any time he wants to," Bobbie told her. "It's just that they don't like to be together. But I need them both. I don't want the kids in my bunk to know about us. And then maybe if they do both come they will love each other and get married again."

Maggie listened quietly as Bobbie went on. She felt sorry for her and yet she didn't know what she could do to help. It must be awful to have only one parent at a time. But maybe Bobbie was right. Maybe they would get married again. Certainly they wouldn't like it if Bobbie ran away from camp.

"Just one thing," Maggie said to her. "I want you to promise me something. Promise me you won't go running off until you talk it over with me."

"Well—" Bobbie was hesitant. "If they won't both

come then I have to do something big that will be sure
to make them come, don't you see?" Bobbie explained.
"Please be my friend and don't tell on me," she pleaded.

"Sure, I'm your friend," Maggie answered. "And you
have to be my friend too. So promise me . . ."

"I promise," Bobbie said very solemnly. "I like you."
And Bobbie gave her a hug.

It made Maggie feel good inside to have Bobbie do
that, and she jumped gaily off the rock. "Come on,
friend, I'll race you to the letter box." And the two of
them were off.

That good feeling didn't last very long for Maggie,
however. Although she was with her bunk mates most
of the time—getting up in the morning, at meals, right
through activities until they went to bed at night—
she still felt she hardly knew them. It wasn't only that
the other girls were old campers and she was new. But
in other ways they seemed so strange to her that she
never felt able to say what she was thinking and the
girls thought she was quiet and reserved. But how could
they know what she was really like when she didn't act
like herself or even feel like herself? Most of the time
she was too lonesome and homesick to care.

In the morning after breakfast, when the girls went
to clean up their bunks, Maggie would do her job as
quickly as possible and then spend the rest of the time
writing letters. The cleaning jobs were rotated so the
girls each had a turn. One day Maggie would sweep,
one day she would empty the wastebasket, another day
polish the lavatory, and another get the fuzz out of the
corners. The two other jobs they all took turns at were
dusting and decorating. When it came to Maggie's turn
to decorate she looked about thoughtfully. When Beth
had done it she had folded all the extra blankets at the

foot of the beds in a fancy way. Carol had picked a few wild flowers for each girl to wear and they all looked gay and cheerful. Maggie wondered what she could do now that it was her turn. She looked around as the others were making their beds and doing their assigned chores. Then she wandered outside. All about were tall pine trees pungently fragrant. Suddenly Maggie wondered if something could be done with the pine? It ought to make the bunk look well. The girls were all eager to make Bunk Five the best-looking bunk in camp. And then an idea came to Maggie in a flash. Why not make a sign with pine boughs to decorate it, and use more pine boughs in the bunk?

"Would it be all right with you," she asked the girls as she went inside again, "if we gave our bunk a name and then made a decorated sign for it? We could call it 'Pine Inn' or something like that . . ."

"Not bad," Julie and Val both chimed in.

"Yeah," Carol spoke slowly. "Only let's get a really good name. 'I Pine for You' or 'Pine Camp.'"

"I know—'Five in the Pines,'" Beth exclaimed.

"But that would leave one of us out," Maggie answered. "We may be Bunk Five but there are six of us in it,"—unless I go home she thought to herself. "There's an old song that was popular on the radio this spring, *In a Mountain Greenery*, what about calling our bunk that?"

"Yes—what's the matter with that?" Val wanted to know. "I like it."

"Me too," Julie added. "That's the best yet. Let's vote on it."

When it was all settled Maggie went to work.

There was a square of wood, with Bunk 5 printed on it, hanging over the door. She took it down and found the other side was nice and clean. Abbey took her to Miss Todd in senior Bunk One. Toddy, as the girls called her, was the arts and crafts counselor, and she got paint and helped Maggie with the printing. Toddy wanted to help her draw pine boughs too but Maggie said, "No, I think we can use real fresh greens for that. I'll just take it like this. The printing looks swell. Is it safe to hang it yet?"

"As long as you don't touch it," Toddy told her. "So it won't smudge. But it won't drip."

"Thanks a lot," Maggie said. "I don't know what it would have looked like without your help . . ." and off she dashed, back to her bunk to finish the job. There was a lot to do before inspection time.

She borrowed a scout knife from Abbey and cut the prettiest branches she could find of cedar, balsam and fir and then twined them together all around the edges of the sign. She put more pine along the ledges where the sides of the bunk met the screening. She was the last one through with her job and the girls were urging her to hurry as Miss Wright approached for inspection.

Beth went to hold the door open for her. Miss Wright looked up at the sign admiringly. The girls stood at attention by their beds as she walked through, noticing how orderly and clean everything looked. "Gold star today," Miss Wright told them. "This is the nicest-looking bunk in camp today. Keep it up."

"Yea!"

"Yippee!"

"Goody!" All the girls were thrilled. As Miss Wright went out after putting a gold star on their inspection chart, they crowded out after her to admire their new sign—"In a Mountain Greenery"—its green letters outlined with yellow, with the fresh greens around it in attractive profusion.

"Good job, Maggie," they told her, and Maggie glowed with pride. But Beth chimed in with, "Well, Maggie will learn someday. But by the time she goes home, she'll get the hayseed out of her pigtails." All Maggie's happiness melted away. If only she could talk to Mom and Daddy, they'd understand. Sometimes she didn't think she could wait for parents' week end. A gold star from Miss Wright wasn't as nice as a big hug on Daddy's lap, or one of her nice long talks with Mother while they worked together. She remembered how often she had teased Mommy to tell her of the days when she was a little girl and went to camp. And now that Maggie herself was at camp she didn't like it. The day before she left home, Mommy had said, "It will be lonesome here without you, Magpie. But you'll be so busy having fun with a crowd of girls that we'll be happy for you."

Maggie had asked, "Will the girls like me? What will I do if I'm homesick?"

And Mommy had answered her, "If you have time to be homesick, just sit down and write me a long letter as though you were right here talking to me, and that will help."

Maggie went back into the bunk now that inspection was over. She didn't feel like being with the girls. Not one of them had said a word about Beth's mean remarks. She would stay here and write that long letter. Even as she thought about it she choked back the tears —she didn't want the girls to see her cry, she didn't feel friendly enough to let them know. When Julie came back in for something Maggie ran into the bathroom.

That was a safe refuge till they all went to the ball field.

She hated to admit that she didn't like camp, that she wasn't happy. She hoped Mommy and Daddy wouldn't be disappointed in her. But they had said she could come home if she didn't like it. She had never felt so bad in her whole life before. The tears rolled down her cheeks faster and faster so that it was hard to keep from blotting her letter. Just then Paulie walked in.

"Well, how come you're here? Aren't you scheduled for activities this morning?" she asked.

"Yes, but I needed to write a letter home." Maggie couldn't look up as she talked. She was afraid Miss Paul would see her red eyes, the tears rolling down her cheeks.

"Tell you what," Paulie said. "You finish your letter, and I'll go get permission from Brownie to start swimming a little early and you and I can get some extra practicing in. We've been slowed up a lot by the swimming tests. Now that we're all through with them I have more time. You have the makings of a good swimmer and with some coaching and practice you'll get there fast. Besides, I'm hoping once you get your white cap you'll come out for crew. We need good sturdy girls like you—and you'll love it, I know."

Paulie couldn't have said anything to please Maggie more, and she was able to end her letter on a happier note than she had begun with. She had planned to swallow her pride and say she didn't think she could last here for the summer. She had been going to ask if she could go home with her parents when they came up to visit, but in her eagerness to be a good swimmer, Maggie decided to postpone the request.

She had never seen people swim like Paulie and Brownie and some of the senior campers. She had to admit they were even better than Mommy, and Mommy was the best swimmer Maggie had known before. It was one of the reasons she had wanted so much to come to camp, to learn to swim like Mommy. Beth was wonderful in the water too. Maggie always spent part of swimming period watching the others. They could dive in swift and straight, skimming the surface of the water, and start swimming even before they came to the end of their dive. Arms and legs worked together rhythmically, propelling them forward with great speed.

"The Australian crawl," Paulie said, "is the hardest stroke to learn but the fastest and easiest to do once you have mastered it." She was explaining it to Maggie on the pier.

Maggie decided she would never be satisfied till she learned to do the crawl. She would work hard and learn fast—maybe by the time her parents came. When the rest of the camp assembled for swimming about a half hour later they were surprised to see Maggie in the water already.

"Hey, how come?" Beth yelled at her. "You're not allowed to go in the water like that. You'll be beached!" Beth sounded triumphant about it but Brownie heard her.

"No, Beth," Brownie told her. "We need other good swimmers besides you. And if you pay more attention to yourself and less to Maggie we'll all have a better time."

Maggie tried to avoid Beth whenever she could, but it was pretty hard since they were in the same bunk.

Maggie grew quieter than ever so she wouldn't say things that Beth could squelch. But every time Maggie thought she had learned something or gotten somewhere Beth was right there to make a dig.

Maggie managed to keep herself busy in free time by reading her mail over and over and writing lots of letters. She wrote a letter home every day and she wrote Ann and Sally as soon as she got a letter from them, at least once a week. It was hard to write to them because she was too proud to tell them how she felt about camp. And yet she had to write because that was the only certain way to get letters back from them.

Chapter Four

MAGGIE PRACTICED HER SWIMMING IN ALL KINDS OF ODD moments. She would walk to meals doing the arm motion of the crawl. She had learned to do a good dive, the side stroke and the breast stroke. Across her bed during rest hour she would work on the flutter kick. And whatever stroke she was doing she would try putting her face in the water and then bringing it up for a breath. It was the third week of camp now and she was working hard to master the requirements for a white cap.

"Friday night we celebrate Miss Wright's birthday," Paulie told her one day out at the float. "We're going to have an Indian pageant here at the Lake. So if you feel like taking your white cap test before then . . ."

"Do you think I could pass yet?" Maggie asked seriously. She remembered how Beth had bragged when she had gotten her white cap again. She had made it quite clear that no one in the bunk was nearly ready except herself. She had said very pointedly to Maggie she would be lucky if she could take the test by the end of summer.

Maggie was surprised therefore when Paulie said to her now, "Sure you could pass it. After all you could swim clear across the lake if you wanted to, couldn't you? And your side stroke is just as good as your breast stroke now. Let's see you do a surface dive."

Maggie promptly dived off the float into the water. As soon as she came up she swam back toward the float and executed a surface dive right there as neat and precise as one would want to see. Before the water was out of her eyes she asked, "Was that all right?"

"Fine," Paulie told her. "You've never done better. You can do it if you want to, can't you, Maggie?"

"Oh, I really want to." Maggie spoke so earnestly it made Paulie pay special attention. "That's the only reason I'm staying," Maggie bubbled on, encouraged by the counselor's sympathetic attitude. "If it weren't for learning how to swim and getting ready for my white cap test I would have asked to go home long ago."

"But, Maggie," Paulie interrupted. "You wouldn't want to go home without giving camp a fair trial. It's true you didn't know anyone when you came here. You didn't have friends. But next year when you come back it will be different. The first time at anything is always strange. Have you ever been away from home before?"

"No." Maggie was thoughtful as she answered. "No, I never have been. But it's not only that. The girls all seem so—I don't know how to say it—so different than I am. They know things and do things I don't know

44

anything about. Half the time I don't even understand them . . ."

"That's because you don't know them well enough yet. You haven't found out about them underneath. There are some pretty nice girls in your bunk. You wait till the end of the summer and then let's talk about it again. What do you say?"

Maggie nodded halfheartedly. If she was still here at the end of summer. If she didn't go home with her family after their visit here. The thought of Bobbie flashed into her mind then. Hadn't she said almost the same thing to Bobbie? Bobbie had wanted to go away from here too. Bobbie hadn't been happy at first either, but for another reason. She knew the girls and the camp, and she had a sister here. For Maggie it was different. She was all alone. And then Maggie had to laugh in spite of herself. After all she didn't have the kind of problem Bobbie and Julie had. Her parents weren't divorced. They were both coming to see her. She couldn't help feeling warm inside when she thought about that. She would get her white cap before they came and then she would be ready to leave.

"Maggie Lowell!" She heard her name being called from the pier. She turned around and swam her best crawl to get there in a hurry. She had been struggling all morning to get the breathing to work with her arm motion and the kick. Somehow she hadn't been able to get it right. But this time it clicked. She skimmed through the water so fast and so easily that she surprised herself as well as those who were watching her.

"Maggie Lowell." It was Brownie who had called her, Brownie who was standing on the edge of the pier, her megaphone and whistle in hand, waiting for her. "I can hardly believe what I see. Are you the same girl who three short weeks ago didn't know one stroke from another? If I remember I called you a fish then. Now I think you're a whale!" She laughed. "I called you in to see when you thought you'd be ready to take your white cap. Now I see you are ready. Want to take it this afternoon?"

Brownie didn't have to wait for the words. The answer was plain in Maggie's face. "Why don't you go out now," Brownie suggested, "and rest up for this afternoon?"

When she got back to her bunk for rest hour Maggie was so excited she could hardly stay still. She couldn't help telling the others, "I'm going to try for my white cap this afternoon."

"That's super," Carol said. "You'll pass it. Brownie wouldn't let you take it if she wasn't pretty sure of you. That's the way she is. I wanted to take mine and she said to practice up a few more days. So she must feel sure of you if she'll let you try."

Then Julie spoke up. "You really have improved, Maggie. I saw you swim to the dock when Brownie called you. You look just as good as Beth does. Now we have two good swimmers in our bunk."

Maggie couldn't help looking over at Beth when Julie said that. She was sure Beth would be angry. But Beth was lying down with her eyes closed. Maggie didn't know whether she was asleep or whether she just didn't want to hear.

"Yeah," Carol put in. "You'll probably get to go on some overnights . . ."

"Quiet Bunk Five!" They were all startled to hear Toddy, who had rest hour duty, call in at the door. Val got up from her bed to tiptoe to the bathroom and on her way she clasped her hands in a good luck gesture to Maggie. Why, the girls really cared. Maggie was pleased and more eager to get her white cap than ever.

46

Not only for herself now, but because her bunk mates wanted it too.

When she came back late in the afternoon, still wearing her white cap because she was so proud of it, the girls were all there to greet her. She didn't remember that they had made a fuss when Beth got her cap after taking the test again. But probably they had celebrated when Beth first got her white cap last year. They had picked her a bouquet of flowers, and only Beth was standoffish and had little to say.

It was only later that Maggie realized the real reason the other girls were so pleased to have someone in their bunk besides Beth win her white cap. When they were getting ready for supper Carol said, "Do you still feel so superior, Miss Morgan, about being the best swimmer in the bunk?"

This time Beth had to face it, she couldn't pretend to be asleep. "You just can't stand it, Carol, to have me do everything better than you do. Thank goodness I'm not so dopey."

That evening when they went to the Ranch, Mickey Fisher got up to work out the plans for Miss Wright's birthday. Maggie had occasion to be proud of herself all over again. Each girl was being assigned her role. Carol, who sang beautifully, was to lead the chorus on the pier. Julie was fire tender at the front of the wigwam. Val was going to be one of the dancers and Beth was one of the four girls in camp who would be Miss Wright's guard of honor. Maggie was given a coveted place in the war canoe! The others looked at her enviously.

The next day she reported for practice in the big war canoe. Maggie had always thought you just got into a canoe and paddled, much like going into the water to swim. But quickly she saw there was more to it than that. There was a way, a right way, to manage a canoe too. There were eight girls in the war canoe, eight water warriors, they were called.

She learned that the bow was the front, and the stern, from which the canoe was steered, was the back. She learned that port was the left side of the canoe facing front, and starboard the right. And also that good canoeists always used these words. She learned how to get into the canoe properly, climbing in at the bow and holding onto the gunwales until she got to her place. She thought the brace was a narrow little seat but she saw the other girls perch on one knee and use the brace as a backrest.

The scramble for costumes, rehearsals and practice kept everyone in camp so busy they hardly had time to find out how the others were getting along. At the dress rehearsal Maggie had to pay strict attention to all her newly acquired tricks, so she wouldn't make a mistake. Every now and then, however, she did glance around. She was impressed with what she saw, at how beautiful it looked. Especially she watched the other war canoe, exactly like the one she was in. Eight paddles started from a rest position across the canoe, they all went up overhead at the same time and in the same way, then dipped silently into the water to send the canoe skimming along. Her canoe was doing the same thing, she realized. They were like a chorus of well-trained dancers, precise and accurate, alike in every motion.

As the rehearsal came to an end, Ann Mason who paddled stern in her canoe said to them, "We did a good job for a new crew. Let's do as well tonight. Let's pull her up now and then we can decorate her." They made garlands of evergreens and fastened them onto the canoe and onto the paddles, and just as they finished Brownie blew her whistle for order.

"Girls," she addressed them all. "Just a few words before I turn this over to Mickey. There will be a lot of people near the water and on the water in the dark. We must do this safely and well. There is to be absolutely no fooling around and you must pay careful attention to what you are told. For safety's sake any nonsense, such as boat rocking, pushing or unnecessary giggling is out. Anything unexpected may lead to trouble and what we all want is to give Miss Wright a nice party. When you have finished your parts, whether in the canoes, on the float or on the pier, you are to get to land as you have already been told, and you will take your places either behind Miss Wright's dais or back of the tent. This will enable other boats to unload without confusion. Is that clear?"

The whole camp agreed to the instructions. They seemed reasonable and right, Maggie thought. And then Mickey got up to talk. "First off," she said, "we're very lucky to have such clear weather. And we're going to have moonlight too! The rehearsal went off very well and you all seem to know your parts. Supper is early tonight, and after it I suggest you go to your bunks, get into your costumes and assemble at the water's edge, ready to take your places. When you've done your stunt, if your costume is not comfortable you may leave it in the paddle house, and all props can be put there too. But please be careful not to leave things lying around. After the fiesta the whole camp will assemble around the campfire before taps."

"You mean ice cream and cake," some of the seniors called out.

"Did I say no?" Mickey countered. And then changing the subject she said, "I have another announcement. There is a birthday girl in my bunk today. Stand up Bobbie." Bobbie Burnett popped up and as all the girls burst into the birthday song she ran over to Julie and climbed right in her lap.

"Put her on the dais with Miss Wright," one of the older campers called out. "Why should she be ignored?"

"Yes, yes," came many replies. "Wasn't she there last year?" someone asked.

"How about it, Bobbie?" Mickey asked her. "Where would you like to be?"

"With my sister and Maggie," Bobbie answered promptly.

After it was explained to her that they weren't together, she decided she would have more fun with her own bunk, taking part in the dance. As the girls were dismissed, Maggie, Julie and a few others crowded around Mickey to make further plans.

The water fête at night was about the most exciting thing that had ever happened to Maggie. The big canoe slid into the water, and each of the girls, dressed as a warrior, took her place in it. They all had feather head-dresses, braids or slicked-back hair, paint on their faces and colored crepe paper shirts. They had wanted to drape themselves in Indian blankets but Brownie wouldn't allow them to wear blankets on the water. The girls of the chorus on the pier wore them.

When Miss Wright marched up onto the dais prepared for her, the campers saluted their chief with song, story and dance. It all went off smoothly, each group doing its assigned part well. When they sang *Happy Birthday* and then gave three Indian yells Miss Wright invited them all to her party around the camp-fire.

"It was a lovely fête, girls," Miss Wright told them. "I enjoyed every minute . . ."

But she couldn't finish her speech. From out of the woods came a terrific yell. Everyone jumped and turned to see what was happening. It had sounded like a real Indian war whoop. From behind the paddle house the yell came again and then they could see someone running. It was an Indian, racing straight toward them, as swift as an arrow.

Only Maggie, Julie, Val and Mickey Fisher knew about this and they were amused that the girls were almost frightened. But when the "real Indian" reached the light of the fire the girls relaxed. The Indian was Val. Still they didn't know what it was all about until she opened the scroll of paper in her hand and read:

> "Hunting sisters, let me read you,
> Peaceful sisters, I shall tell,
> We have had a celebration,
> We have fêted well.
> Sisters, we have joy to dwell on,
> Sisters, we have something more,
> We have cause for song and laughter
> At the edge of Sunset Water.
> For the moon and stars do tell us
> With their vigil of the time
> Another tribesman came to join us
> Just ten years ago today.
> Have we not good cause for cheering?
> Hunting sisters, heed me well.
> Another notch upon our totem,
> For Bobbie's birthday let us yell.
> Our chief doth share this merrily
> So Bobbie too can happy be,
> On this great day. Let's give a cheer!
> To Bobbie and Miss Wright we say
> Hooray!"

The whole camp, counselors and girls, burst forth with applause and then Kate Simon, the head cheerleader, called for the loudest, biggest cheer of the day. Miss Wright invited Bobbie to sit up on the dais with her for the party. They didn't have to wait in line for they were the guests of honor and they were served their ice cream and cake first.

After the party Julie and Maggie walked Bobbie back to her bunk. "It was just wonderful!" Bobbie exclaimed. "I didn't know it could be so exciting. I was really scared when I heard the screeches. Don't you wish you had your birthday at camp, Maggie?"

Maggie was pleased that Bobbie really sounded happy. Once again she began to compare her own misery to Bobbie's and she had to admit to herself that she had enjoyed today. The whole Indian fête, having a part in it along with all the others, had been fun for her. It was something that in a million years would never have happened to her at home. She skipped back to her own bunk feeling happy too.

As she went to bed it dawned on her that in another week she would see her mother and father. She could hardly wait for them to get here. She would be able to leave camp now with a little better feeling about it. She wanted so to see them, to show them how she could swim and paddle. She even smiled as she fell asleep, thinking how happy she would be next week.

At lunch the following day, Brownie called eight girls' names, and asked to see them at the paddle house after rest hour. Maggie couldn't imagine what was up. Maggie, Carol and Beth were the only ones from their bunk, the others were all from older bunks, and a few were seniors. That was the surprise part. That was what made them all so curious. At rest period Carol asked Abbey, "Have we been bad or something?"

"Have you a guilty conscience?" Abbey laughed. "You have a pleasant surprise in store for you. Don't worry. You'll like what Brownie has to tell you."

"A canoe trip!" Beth suggested and then she said, "Only that wouldn't include Carol. She can't go on a trip with us. She's not a white cap."

Carol lamented, "I probably never will be either. I'm not allowed to dive and how can you be a white cap if you can't dive?"

It seemed as though rest hour would never end. Maggie thought back over every time Brownie had called her name, and each time something nice had happened. Her first swimming test, then her white cap test, then a place in the war canoe. She wasn't scared any more. Something nice would happen this time too.

"All the paddling lessons we can give you won't help as much as this trip we're planning for you," Brownie told them later. "This is a mixed age trip, four seniors and four intermediate campers. If the weather holds you can leave camp after breakfast on Wednesday, go down the lake to the carry and into Big Rockwood Lake. You are not due back in camp until Thursday evening, any time before eight o'clock. A two-day, one-night trip—so you ought to have fun. Paulie, Toddy and Martha will be your counselors. Four canoes, three in each except for the supply canoe. Paulie will help those who have never been out before, tell you what you need and how to pack. You'd better get together Tuesday evening to make your plans."

Brownie let them think about it for a few minutes and then, just before dismissing them, asked, "Any questions?"

Carol was fidgeting and nervous as she asked, "Is

there a mistake about me, Brownie? I don't have a white cap . . ."

"I know, Carol, and you probably won't be able to get one if you can't dive. But you are a good swimmer and we think you deserve the chance." Brownie laughed as she saw Carol's relief. "Wouldn't it be awful to make such a mistake?" Brownie laughed again.

There were so many things to be done that the days sped by on wings. Beth had been on a trip last year so she knew what it was all about and what to expect. But Carol and Maggie were new at it and though Carol had seen girls pack for an overnight it was the first time she had done it herself. Maggie was intrigued with each step.

Carol and Maggie spent every spare minute on the water, learning to steer and to use a canoe with skill. "If you sit up straight," Paulie said, "your back won't get as tired. And you look so much nicer." She laughed as they straightened up.

Paulie had four canoes out practicing now, one girl in each. She was teaching them how to maneuver by themselves, how to shift seats, to turn unexpectedly, what happened when you were alone in the stern, that it was better to go into the bow and paddle stern from the bow of the canoe. All of a sudden, with a great splash Maggie found herself in the water. She came up bewildered, her hair streaming in her eyes, her clothes sticking to her, and she looked about anxiously. What had happened? Her canoe had turned over! Would they let her go on the trip? That was the first thought that flashed through her head. She noticed then that Carol was still in her canoe but she had no paddle. And Beth and Paulie were paddling away. Beth was laughing as hard as she could but Paulie was watching intently.

Maggie got hold of her paddle and swam over to

hold on to the side of her canoe. She didn't even stop to think about it, she just did it and started to swim for shore. Then she looked at Paulie questioningly. What was this all about? Was this another of Beth's tricks?

Carol was watching Maggie, and when she saw that Maggie was managing all right she smiled and called, "And what am I supposed to do without a paddle?"

"Here." Maggie left her overturned canoe and started swimming toward Carol with her paddle.

"Let Carol work this out," Paulie stopped her. "What would you do if you lost your paddle on a trip?" she asked.

"Make for shore somehow," Carol answered.

"Go ahead then," and they all watched as Carol leaned across the stern seat and paddled the canoe stern first with her hands.

Meantime Maggie had put her paddle under the braces of her canoe and was pulling it toward shore. When she was nearly in Paulie called, "Wait there.

"You girls know what to do! You reacted beautifully. You'll make fine trippers, I can see that. And we certainly took you unawares, but it's better that way. If you want to have some fun with the capsized canoe before we go in I'll give you about five minutes."

So it was all a plan. It had not been an accident. Paulie and Beth had done it deliberately to see how Maggie and Carol would react in an emergency. They were certainly lucky, Maggie thought, to have done what they did. She didn't realize it was their good judgment much more than their luck that had pleased Paulie. Would things like that happen on the trip? Well, they were leaving in the morning, there wouldn't be long to wait now, Maggie laughed to herself.

Chapter Five

WEDNESDAY MORNING, ON SCHEDULE, THE GIRLS ASsembled at the lake right after breakfast. Maggie came puffing along carrying her blanket roll. Julie had gotten permission to help her and Val was helping Carol. Maggie's shining, eager face matched the rest of her appearance, her hair neat as could be in two pigtails, blue shorts and a white shirt over her bathing suit and sneaks tied together and slung across her shoulders.

By ten o'clock the canoes were all packed and the girls got into their places. With waves and cheers from the girls on shore, and from Miss Wright and Brownie standing on the pier, they started off down the lake. Maggie was paddling bow in the second canoe. Jean Barrett was at stern and Martha was their passenger.

"You take starboard and I'll paddle port for a while," Jean said as they pushed off.

"I'll take the starboard and you'll take the port. We'll be at Lake Rockwood at twilight,"

Maggie sang and they all laughed. The girls went right on singing as they paddled, all kinds of songs—camp songs, school songs, popular songs—and in a short while camp was out of sight. But the four canoes, their bright blue paint shining, stayed close together, close enough to call out to each other, or join in songs.

"Hey, supply canoe, we're getting hungry, what've you got to offer?" Paulie cupped her hands together as she called from the lead canoe.

"Raisins, bananas or oranges," Ethel answered promptly. "We're hungry too."

"Is it lunchtime yet?" Jean asked.

"No, it's just after eleven. We'll stop for a swim later, and then we'll eat lunch," Martha answered. "Isn't this fun? I've never been down the lake this far before, have either of you?"

"I have," Jean told her. "But not on an overnight. We had a motor launch ride down this way, to that point just ahead, last summer. It was our bunk treat and we voted to come down here, cook supper, sit around the campfire and ride back in the launch by moonlight. It was wonderful, but it's even more fun in a canoe."

The four canoes had pulled one alongside the other now. The girls were getting bananas from the supply canoe, and having a rest from paddling while they ate. Maggie was between Ethel, who was bow in the supply canoe, and Peggy, who was bow in the lead. The counselors, who were the passengers, were holding the boats together.

"How about Indian Point for a swim? It's the point beyond the one just ahead of us—about a fifteen-minute paddle," Paulie added.

"Let's go," was the general agreement. With snap and dash the canoes separated and the girls paddled hard. "Stroke, together, stroke." First one canoe, then all four were in unison. The canoes fairly raced along, bumping the ripples with a gentle slapping noise. In what seemed like no time at all they were beaching. First Maggie got out, pulled the boat up a little, then Martha got out and they pulled up some more. Then Jean got out.

"First one in," she yelled as she dropped her shorts and pulled off her shirt.

In a few minutes they were all in the water, gay and carefree, splashing, playing. It was not the same as at camp. There were so few of them here and they had not only left camp behind them, but all routines, all concerns. They were off on a spree! Maggie had never felt anything like this in her whole life before. This is what Mommy must have meant when she used to say, "Camp is like nothing else that I know. It has its own special quality of fun, being with a whole crowd of girls, doing things you can never quite duplicate any place else!" Maggie had remembered those words earlier this summer, but now they really had meaning. She began to understand why Mommy had loved camp.

Supper time at Big Rockwood Lake was even better. They found a camp site with a lean-to. As they un-packed their canoes they joked and giggled. Then the canoes were pulled out of the water and turned over at the edge. In a little clearing back from the beach they made their fireplace, collecting stones for the edge of the fire, firewood and kindling. They used the lean-to to store their supplies. Then they hauled their blanket rolls back under the trees. Each girl tried out her place for smoothness, to find where the sticks and stones were. They looked like a family of beavers burrowing away, but they sounded like laughing hyenas. They wanted to get their sleeping places ready before dark, and they were trying to make them at least as comfortable as the wooden floor of the lean-to. They had been firm about sleeping in the open, so when Carol pulled out a pebble from under her roll they all went into fresh peals of laughter.

When everyone seemed satisfied that her spot was as smooth as a Beauty Rest mattress they got ready for supper. Linda, Dorothy and Beth were elected cooks for the first meal. They made supper over the open fire. The whiffs that came to the others as they stood waiting started them cheering the cooks on. First they had tomato soup, then steak, with potatoes baked in the fire, and string beans. They made hot cocoa and spoon biscuits with jelly for dessert. Eleven of them made a nice cozy circle around the campfire, eating leisurely, talking and laughing, relishing every second.

Finally Toddy spoke up. "Who wants to help me with kitchen cleanup? And some of you can collect enough wood for the evening before it gets too dark. Then we'll be able to relax."

"I will, I will," came several offers. Ethel, Peggy, Jean and Toddy set about washing the pots and pans in the lake, using sand to scrub them clean, burning garbage, and putting things away. Carol, Maggie, Dorothy and Martha went wood-gathering. When they finished they walked along the shore, joining the others to watch the sunset over the lake. They looked back to see the thin curl of smoke that marked their fire. "We'd better go back and watch it," Martha warned. "It's been pretty dry and we need to be careful."

"Are you tired from the big paddle?" Paulie wanted to know.

"Oh, no! It was wonderful. We could start right out again," they informed her.

"'Cept I'm having such a good time I wouldn't want to change a thing," Maggie said.

"Look!" Paulie was pointing into the woods. "Blueberries!" she exclaimed. "Let's pick some—we can have them for breakfast. Maggie, run back and get a few cups, will you? We can make blueberry pancakes." Paulie was already starting to pick, and in a minute her hands were almost full.

Maggie came back in a moment with five cups and they soon had enough berries to nearly fill them. "We have treasure, we have gold," they were shouting. "Don't know how I can think of food now, after that wonderful dinner, but I guess we'll be hungry after sleeping out and an early morning swim," Paulie said.

"Can we swim before breakfast?" Linda wanted to know.

"Sure, silly," Beth answered. "How would we get washed if we didn't?"

"On an overnight we make all the rules together," Paulie told them. "Why, we can swim whenever we feel like it. If you want to swim before you go to sleep tonight I think it's warm enough. And," her voice dropped, "if we do it quietly we can go without suits."

Maggie was sure this was the way a mermaid must feel, or a real fish, light and easy, as though water was her natural home. Each thing that happened on this trip was more wonderful than the last. What would happen next, she wondered, and then realized it was time for bed.

The girls had put their towels and pajamas across the canoes, ready for them when they came out of the water. To their surprise, they felt damp. "Dew!" they exclaimed, and laughed at their mistake.

"Me for the fire." Peggy ran over to it. "Let's build it up a bit till we get dried out." They stood around it, tingling from the swim, getting one side dry and then turning to dry out on the other.

"I could eat a piece of candy right now," Jeannie spoke up. "Has anybody got some?"

When no one answered Peggy suggested, "Couldn't we make fudge? I could go for some. We have cocoa, sugar and milk. We could make it in the water pail over the fire. The pail is all scrubbed. . . ."

"Wonderful," Toddy spoke up to the others' amazement. The counselors were certainly being swell sports, Maggie thought.

Before anyone had a chance to say more the flashlights were on and the lean-to was bright with their light. "Here's the cocoa." Peggy had it in one hand, the pail in the other.

"Here's the sugar and a can of milk," and they started to mix. When it was ready to go on the fire they took a big stick and put it through the pail handle to hold it right over the flames. Carol held one end and Dorothy the other. Maggie ran down to the lake for a cup of cold water to test the fudge.

"Do we have to wait till it's cold to eat it?" Jeannie asked. "I could spoon it. Hot fudge! Sounds divine!"

"Yeah," Beth agreed. "Then we won't have to wait so long."

There never was a batch of fudge like that one. In the woods on the shore of a lake, around a campfire after a swim—that was the way to make fudge. Any other way couldn't possibly be as good.

"What time is it?" Carol asked, licking the last of her portion from her spoon.

"Time to get to sleep," Paulie answered, glancing at her watch. "Almost eleven o'clock. We'd better sleep fast because you'll find we wake up early."

After a few grunts and amused groans while squirming around on the hard ground to get comfortable, they settled down to sleep quickly. It seemed to Maggie she had just closed her eyes when she opened them again. But it couldn't be! It was daylight already. The fire was going! Carol, who had slept next to her, was already up and about. Maggie saw the heavy mist rising off the lake as she stretched herself to get rid of the kinks. Then a broad smile spread across her face. Another wonderful day. And with that she jumped out of bed too.

"Hey, sleepyhead," Carol greeted her. "We're just waiting for you, Paulie and Peggy, so we can have a swim. How did you sleep?"

"Fast," Maggie laughed. "I didn't know a thing till just now. And you?" She looked at Carol and the others.

There were all kinds of answers. Linda had found herself sliding downhill. Dorothy had kept rolling over and bumping into Toddy.

"Have you been up long?" came a sleepy voice from deep in one of the bedrolls. "What's the hurry?" It was Peggy, and then they heard Paulie answer her. "I know, they're all waiting for blueberry pancakes.

Let's go," and like a flash she was up and the first one in the water.

They were all pleased to see they didn't have to wear suits in the water now either. "After all," Paulie told them, "it's only a little after six. And if anyone were on the lake they couldn't see us for the mist. Besides we'll have dry suits to put on when we come out."

Some of the girls took soap into the water. "May I borrow some," Maggie asked, "to get this smudge off my arm?"

"Go get your own," Beth snapped back at her.

"You still can't take it, can you, Beth?" Carol said. "Maggie isn't hurting you. Why do you have to be so unpleasant?"

"None of your business," and Beth swam away.

Martha threw her soap over to Maggie so she didn't have to get out of the water. "Don't you mind, Maggie," she said. "The rest of us love you anyway. And Beth will learn."

Maggie didn't mind this time. She was having such fun and the others were all so nice that she really felt like one of the girls. She had laughed more since yesterday than all the rest of the time she had been at camp. She washed off her smudge, gave the soap back to Martha, and went to help Paulie make pancakes.

"I'll never forget this," she told Paulie. "If you hadn't helped me with swimming and canoeing, if you hadn't spurred me on I wouldn't have been here. Isn't that an awful thought?"

"Let's ban it," Paulie laughed. " 'Cause you're here and doing a fine job. So cheer up, little one, and you'll be recommended for more trips."

That gave Maggie a special glow that stayed with

her for a long time. The rest of the day was wonderful anyway, but with Paulie's praise as well, Maggie was the gayest, funniest one in the group.

"I hope we all go on another trip together," Peggy said as they neared camp that evening. "This is a wonderful group. I thought it would be dull to go with intermediate campers. But you're all good scouts and it doesn't matter whether you're seniors or not." That coming from a senior camper was the ultimate in compliments.

"And we thought you might be stuck up and snooty about us," Jeannie said. "How about it, Paulie? Can you put us all together again?"

Paulie wasn't to be pinned down to any promises. "We'll see. You know part of good camping is to get along well with others, so we have to think about that, too. I'll tell you one thing, however. I never went out on a nicer trip, or one that was more fun. And I've been going out on them for three years now. So you can all feel good about it and look forward to another one soon."

As Maggie climbed into her bunk that night, tired but happy, with a wonderful sunburn and a fine feeling deep inside, she thought to herself, "If I could go out on trips all the time I would stay at camp. But when I wake up tomorrow I'll just have one day and night to wait. Then the next wake-up will be when Mommy and Daddy come." She hugged herself with joy at the thought.

All day Friday Maggie and the other girls in Bunk Five were busy cleaning, straightening up, getting ready for their visitors. They were determined to look their best. They unpacked their trunks and put everything back as neatly as possible. They scrubbed, polished, and shined everything in sight, they got fresh and fragrant pine to redecorate the ledges and their sign. By the end of the day they were admiring each other's efforts and agreeing they had done their best and now they were ready.

"And you worked as hard as any of us, Carol," Val told her. "That was very decent of you since your parents can't come."

"Well, why not?" she asked impishly. "I've had fun with you and I must say we do look super. I think I'll take a picture 'cause the bunk will never look this way again. Clear out of the way, kids," she yelled as she went for her camera.

After she had taken pictures with her own camera and then snapped some for Maggie and the others, she lined them all up outside. "I'll get another like this tomorrow," she laughed. "We can call it before and after." They all knew what she meant for their best clothes were being kept in readiness for the visitors, and they had not even stopped to clean themselves up in their eagerness to get the bunk in order.

Right after breakfast on Saturday Carol got them all together again. "Fix yourselves up before you start making beds," she told them. "I want to get the pictures before the excitement starts." She ran to get Toddy who had promised to snap the picture on each girl's camera. Toddy would do a good job and then Carol could be in the picture as well as Abbey.

"Can you get our sign in?" Maggie asked, as they were all in a huddle at the door of the bunk.

"I can get the sign, but Abbey needs to move in closer. I only see half her face." Toddy got them just the way she wanted and snapped two pictures with each camera, just to be sure.

Then they all rushed in to make the beds. Miss Wright had announced that parents would begin arriving early as many had reached Lakeville the night before.

Before inspection started Maggie heard it! The woodpecker whistle sounded way off in the distance. She stopped still for a second, her face getting pale, and then she heard it again, nearer this time, no mistaking it. Without a word she dashed out of the bunk like a streak of lightning. It happened so fast the others didn't realize what it was.

"Mommy! Mommy! Daddy!" The words started with a scream and ended in a sob as she flew into her father's arms. Maggie didn't know why, when she was so happy to see them, she burst into tears like that. But she just couldn't stop crying as Daddy held her up in his arms. She kissed first one and then the other over and over again.

"Maggie, you look good to us, even crying," Daddy exclaimed. "Even with those red eyes. Let's have a good look." He took out his pocket handkerchief to help her but she couldn't stop.

"Oh, Mommy!" She sobbed it over and over, gulping back new waves of tears, holding on for dear life.

Brownie came along then. "I can guess who you are." She smiled at Mr. and Mrs. Lowell. "Maggie, you don't look like the girl who came home from the Rockwood trip Thursday night. Your daughter is a regular fish, you know. I think we'll send her out on another trip right now so you can have the pleasure of seeing her when she gets back."

That ended the crying spell for Maggie. She took

Daddy's hanky, wiped the tears away and linked her arms through both her parents'. She walked along with them toward her bunk, chattering away for all she was worth. All kinds of things spilled out. "I went on the overnight to Big Rockwood Lake, four canoes— hello, Martha—Martha was one of our counselors on the trip—and I want you to come right to the bunk to meet—hello, Miss Strang, she's the camp nurse—Carol's parents can't come because they live so far away— there's Val, emptying our wastebasket—we haven't had inspection yet. If you hadn't gotten here early I think I would have died. Gee," the words came out with such a sigh that Mr. and Mrs. Lowell recognized how important they were. "Gee, how I've missed you. See our bunk sign 'In a Mountain Greenery' from that old song. We were the first in camp to get a sign up. Here's where I live. I never thought I would stay here this long. . . ." Maggie was wound up like a tight spring as she talked on, not waiting for answers or questions, just spilling her heart out.

Chapter Six

NOT UNTIL THE SWIMMING WHISTLE BLEW AT ELEVEN o'clock could Maggie let go of her mother and father. She hung onto them as though they might disappear. But she was eager to show off her swimming, how she could dive in head first, her strokes and all she had learned. It took her less time to get into her bathing suit than to tell about it and then she walked her parents to the swimming area to wait for the signal to go in.

Lots of the mothers and fathers were there now. "This is my daddy," "This is my mother," "This is the new girl in our bunk, Maggie Lowell," and the introductions were made all around.

Julie walked over to the group with her father. Maggie couldn't help but feel sorry for her, and Bobbie too.

They had wanted both their parents to be here, they had tried every way they could think of to get them together again. And until the last minute they had hoped. Mr. Burnett had answered the letter Maggie had helped Bobbie write with his promise to be here today. But not until yesterday's mail had their mother finally told them she couldn't make it. They had felt badly and Bobbie had cried, but at least they had their father here. Some of the girls had no one.

"Has everyone come yet?" Julie asked.

"I saw Beth with her folks," Maggie told her. "But I haven't seen Val yet."

Julie and her father went off in search of Bobbie.

"Are all the children's parents coming?" Maggie's daddy asked.

"All but Carol's—she's from Chicago and this is too far for them. I wouldn't come to camp at all if you couldn't come to see me." Just then Carol came along. "Carol," Maggie called to her. "Come meet my family."

"You must have been out on a canoe trip too," Maggie's mother said. "You two have the most sunburn of anyone I've seen."

"Maggie and I were on the same trip," Carol answered. "It was wonderful. I never had such a good time. Did you tell them all about it?" she asked Maggie.

"She's been talking about nothing else since we got here. And she did manage to tell us you two are pretty good friends, too." Daddy smiled.

"Oh, we are! Maggie's about my best friend in camp." Just then Brownie blew the whistle for all in and Maggie, with a warning to watch, ran to the end of the pier and dived in head first. Maggie was not the only one to put on an exhibition. All the girls were showing off for their parents. There was exhibition swimming and diving all over the place.

Maggie saw her father walk out on the pier. She swam toward him to see what he wanted. "Do you think Mrs. Lowell and I might have a swim?" he asked Brownie.

Maggie held her breath as she waited for the answer. "Why, that would be fine," Brownie answered. "You wouldn't mind going in when the counselors do, would you?"

"We'd love it," Daddy told her. "We're too busy watching our daughter right now. We're both very impressed with your wonderful job," Mr. Lowell said. "Maggie, all the children look very professional to us."

"We're pretty proud of Maggie," Brownie answered. "But it's easy when someone loves the water as much as she does. She seems to have stayed here only for the water sports. Wait till you see her in a canoe."

When the children had finished swimming the counselors went in. After Maggie was dressed again in her best shorts and shirt, she did her hair as neatly as could be and went back to the lake to watch. There were Mommy and Daddy in the water, swimming around with the counselors. She heard Mommy say to Abbey, "This feels wonderful. It brings back all the memories of my childhood when I used to go to camp and love it."

Hers were the only parents in the water, Maggie noticed. She felt very proud of them. All the others were standing about in their dressed-up clothes, waiting for their children or already walking away with them.

All of a sudden Val cried out, "Here they come! This must be them! I think it is!" Maggie turned to look, but Val was watching an airplane in the sky. No, she couldn't mean that. Maggie looked up the road but Val was jumping up and down, her eyes glued on the plane in the air. Maggie stared too. The plane did seem to be coming lower, to be circling. "Is that your family?" she asked, in utter disbelief.

"Yes," Val answered matter-of-factly. "They won't come any other way so I'm lucky it's a nice day. Sure, that's it." She tugged at Abbey who was out of the water now. "That's it, they'll be down in a second. Let's get into the boat."

Abbey floated the big rowboat, she and Val climbed in and started out to meet the lovely silver bird that was just hitting the water. The seaplane taxied in toward shore and Maggie's eyes nearly popped.

"Didn't you know?" Julie was saying. "They came that way last year too. It's their own plane—the Silver Hunter, they call it—and Mr. Hunter pilots it himself. Last year they took us all up for a ride. I hope they do again . . ."

Maggie looked out over the water at Val in amazement. No wonder she hadn't been able to understand. This girl did come from another world, and she wouldn't understand Maggie's world any better than Maggie understood hers. But then, she thought, Carol's parents didn't have a plane or they certainly would have come too. Carol came over just then. "Gee, Maggie, look at your mother and father. Aren't they swell? The only parents up here who went swimming. You're lucky. And they're good swimmers too. I think they're just wonderful."

"Why don't you sit with us at dinner, Carol?" Maggie asked her. "We could all have fun."

When they went in for dinner the tables were arranged so parents could sit with their own children. Mr. Lowell went over to talk to Miss Wright and when he came back he said to Maggie and Carol, "I told Miss Wright we'd like to adopt Carol for the whole week end, and not to have to ask permission to have her sit with us or be with us or go out with us. She said that was fine, so let's eat. Your lake gave me an appetite."

The girls hardly had time to eat, they were so busy singing. Each bunk sang its own song, they all sang the camp songs, and in between were cheers of all kinds—for the visitors, for the ice cream, for everything anyone could think of. It got to be funny after awhile, especially when the seniors started cheering themselves and then the other groups took their cue and did the same.

After the ice cream was served Miss Wright blew her whistle. "I have bad news," she began. Amid the groans that greeted the announcement she went on, "But taps will be later tonight so you really need a good rest hour. The counselors will stay here on the porch to talk to any of the parents who want to see them," she finished, "so you'll know where to look when rest hour is over. This afternoon there will be swimming and boating for those who want it. But you can do as you please until supper. Tonight we have a square dance."

Maggie was undecided. She wanted to go canoeing to show Mommy and Daddy how well she could do it but she also wanted to go for a ride with them. All the girls looked forward to going out with their parents. The Lowells had said they would take Carol, Abbey and anyone else who wanted to crowd in for a ride to their hotel and a treat. Back at the bunk Maggie heard Val announce, "Mother and Father have invited the whole bunk to fly over to Bar Harbor tomorrow for dinner. I hope you'll all come. Maggie and Julie and Beth, if your parents would drive over they could come too."

Maggie's heart leapt to her mouth with excitement. An airplane ride! Would Mommy and Daddy be willing to drive way over there? Maggie was so busy trying to figure out how much she could crowd into one short week end that she jumped when Carol shook her. "Wake up," Carol kept saying. "Rest hour is over."

Maggie and Carol found Mr. and Mrs. Lowell on the dining porch talking to some of the counselors. The girls were impatient to tell all their plans and they hovered over the grown-ups so closely that Mommy turned about, with her arm around Maggie's waist to ask, "What's on your mind, darling? You seem ready to explode or something."

"The Hunters have invited us all to Bar Harbor tomorrow—the girls in our bunk to ride in the plane and you and Daddy to drive over with any other parents from the bunk. Would you? Would you let me go in their plane?"

Daddy turned to her when he heard that. "Well, that's quite a plan! It would be hard to say no to that. But wait a little and let's see. We don't want to be in the way either. . . ."

"But, Daddy," Maggie went on impatiently. "We've got to decide now. If we don't go tomorrow then we should go somewhere now. We have to have one excursion out of camp together—everybody does! And if we don't go somewhere now we can go swimming and boating and take you for canoe rides and show you . . ."

"We won't be in the Hunters' way—they took the whole bunk for a ride last year too," Carol was saying.

"Say yes, Daddy, say yes," Maggie pleaded. "It would be just perfect."

"I think we could, don't you?" he asked Mommy. And Maggie and Carol both concentrated on her.

"Let me get it all straight," Mommy spoke up. "We stay here in camp this afternoon and then drive over to Bar Harbor tomorrow. How far away is that?" she asked.

"Let's ask the Hunters," Carol put in quickly. "There they are now," she exclaimed as she waited for the Lowells to start toward them.

But Val was leading her parents straight to them. Mr. Hunter, as soon as he was introduced, invited them all over again. "We'd love to take the children for a ride tomorrow, weather permitting. And if there's room we can take you too, only we don't know for sure how many will come. But if the plane is full and you wouldn't mind the driving too much, it would be nice to have you join us there. Mrs. Hunter and I both would like it and I guess you know how the kids feel."

The Lowells were good sports about it. "Nothing like this ever happened to me when I went to camp," Mother commented. "And it certainly does sound like fun." She laughed.

The girls set up a cheer, hugging each other and prancing with delight. Tomorrow to Bar Harbor by plane! Today they could swim and paddle and maybe the Lowells would swim with them.

When Brownie and Paulie saw that only about half the camp had come out for swimming they said the Lowells could swim with the children if they wanted. They were as eager as the kids and rushed off to get into their suits. They played tag in the water, raced about and had a generally hilarious time. When Maggie and Carol took a canoe Mommy swam to it and climbed in just like they had had to when they took their white cap tests.

"Gee, look at that!" Carol was impressed. "I'd like to see my mother do that." It was more like a family day at the beach than a swim period at camp. Carol wasn't the only one who admired the Lowells. The other girls swam around and joined in to play and laugh with them too.

When swimming was over Mommy and Daddy said, "We're going back to the hotel now to rest and eat and dress. We'll be back early for the square dance. Maybe you ought to rest a little too." Maggie and Carol walked to the car with them, hating to see them drive off even for a little while.

As they went back to their bunk together at least four girls told Maggie how nice or what fun or how lucky she was to have such parents. Maggie had always taken her family for granted so that it surprised her to have the girls comment. "But, Carol, what would your parents do if they could come?"

"I don't know, but this is my second year here and I never saw parents go swimming and play with us the way yours do. Your mother seems as much like our friend as the counselors'. She's not bossy or strict or trying to be motherly. You know, like telling you it's time to get out of the water and all kinds of stuff like that. And your daddy is more fun than a pack of monkeys. I'll bet Beth's parents won't go to Bar Harbor tomorrow and they probably won't let Beth go either."

When the square dance started they managed to forget everything else. Usually they danced to records but tonight they had a caller from the village. He was on the stage with his violin, ready to begin. The seniors had decorated for the occasion and the girls all wore their prettiest blouses, gay ribbons and dancing shoes. As the first sets were forming Mr. Lowell jumped up and asked Maggie to be his partner and Mrs. Lowell asked Carol.

After the first set in which they danced to *The Gal from Arkansaw,* some of the other parents got up to join in too. They saw what fun the Lowells were having and how much the children enjoyed it. They all squealed with delight when the caller announced their favorite dances. The Ranch was vibrating as they swung into *Pop Goes the Weasel* with gay abandon, faces shining with warmth.

As it got later and the girls knew that taps would be coming any minute they danced harder than ever, hoping Miss Wright would forget. Furtive glances were stolen at watches and Julie whispered to Maggie, "It's nine o'clock already. How late do you think she'll let us stay?"

"Now choose your partners and we'll do *Old Dan Tucker,*" the caller announced. "And listen well, for we'll go from that right into a glorious finish. It's getting late and we haven't done the reel yet. We'll end on that. Do you know Dan?" he asked.

"Old Dan Tucker was a fine old man," the whole camp started to sing.

"That's it," the caller smiled. "A grand right and left. And watch out Old Dan doesn't steal your partner, 'cause that's what this dance is all about."

They danced well and attentively, each of the eight sets that had been going all evening. As the caller fiddled and called the dance the whole camp sang the song. Only no words could be heard. The girls were forming the words with their mouths but they weren't letting any sound pass their lips because they wanted to hear every word the caller said. It looked so funny to the few spectators that some of them laughed right out. When the Old Dan Tucker of each set managed to steal a partner the squeals from the rest of the set were enough to make them laugh anyway.

When they swung into *The Virginia Reel* Carol and Maggie linked arms as soon as they saw the Lowells link theirs. "This is the first dance I've had with your daddy all evening," Mommy giggled. "He's very popular. But then there have only been a few men dancing so I guess they've all been in demand."

No one seemed to mind that the party was over when Miss Wright stood at the door to say goodnight. "There're milk and cookies on the porch," she told them. "Help yourselves."

They had had a wonderful day, a long evening and though it was hard to have such a good time come to an end they were happy in knowing that there was more to come tomorrow. Camp settled down to sleep that night so quickly that Abbey told them in the morning, "We ought to make every night like last night. Think I'll bring that up at the next counselors' meeting."

"Shall we get dressed to go now or later?" Carol asked when she got up. "And what are you going to wear, Val?"

"How many of us are going?" Val wanted to know. "Let's see, are you with us, Julie?"

"Gee, I can't go," she lamented. "We'd have to take Bobbie and my father says it's too much and he'd rather stay right here." Julie felt sad about it and so did Val.

"You'll come, won't you, Beth?" Val asked.

"My parents came up by train so they can't drive

over to Bar Harbor. I'm staying here with them," she said with no expression.

"Couldn't they ride over with my parents?" Maggie asked.

"That's just like you, Maggie," Carol couldn't help saying. "Why don't you ask them, Beth?"

"Thanks, but we have other plans," Beth replied as she walked into the bathroom, slamming the door behind her.

"What's she on her high horse for?" Julie asked.

"She's probably jealous," Carol answered.

"Gee," Val exclaimed, counting on her fingers. "Maybe your mother and father could go in the plane with us. There're the three of us and Carol and Maggie, that's five, and your family would make seven and in a pinch we can hold eight." Maggie was holding her breath as Val went on. "I'll phone up and ask. But I'm sure it will be all right."

"What about Abbey?" Maggie didn't want to plan it and then be disappointed, so she was trying to think of everything.

"Even so, that would only be eight," Val countered.

After breakfast the three girls got busy fixing themselves for the great excursion. They selected their best clothes, spent a long time brushing and arranging their hair, and tried on all each others' jewelry, looking for the best combination they could find. Maggie wore her cotton print dress, brushed out her hair and wore it hanging loose with a silver barrette that belonged to Val. She wore her own heart-shaped locket and an Indian bracelet that she borrowed from Julie.

Val wore a white linen sun-back dress with a plaid belt and a plaid purse to match. She put a white tennis shield on her head with a pin on it to dress it up. Her hair was short and stayed neat with the cap on. Carol had only the dress she traveled in, a printed sun-back with a bolero jacket and she wore beads, a ring, a bow in her hair and carried a purse and gloves. Val gave them each a dab of toilet water and they felt very elegant as they waited for the Lowells and the Hunters to arrive together. Val had arranged by telephone for that. The plane was still anchored out in the lake, just beyond the swimming area.

They waited near the entrance and when Maggie spied her family's car the three of them started jumping up and down, yelling, "We're ready! We're ready, let's go!" After greetings and kisses all the way around they went down to the lake. Abbey rowed them out to the plane in two trips. The nearer they got the bigger the plane looked and all the Lowells, Mommy and Daddy and Maggie, were busy taking everything in.

Mr. Hunter got out of the boat first, climbed onto the wing and unlocked the door of the cabin. He helped the others out of the boat, onto the wing and into the plane. "Aren't you coming along, Miss Wittmer?" he asked Abbey as she was pushing off.

"No, I can't," she replied regretfully, "much as I'd love it. I have two girls staying in camp and several other counselors are off. But have a lovely time. And happy landings." She waved as she started rowing back to shore.

Maggie was speechleess! She hadn't quite figured out what to expect in the plane but certainly it was nothing like she might have imagined. The cabin was fixed like a room. There were two big built-in settees that doubled for beds if need be, Val told her. There were small chairs and some tables and pictures on the wall between the big windows. They even had a little bathroom and a small electric stove with a few groceries stored on shelves above it.

"This really is fine," Arthur Lowell told his host. "We've never seen anything like this and it's quite a treat. I thought at first you had one of those two-passenger planes and I couldn't figure out how you'd do it."

"We started with an air coupé," Jack Hunter told him. "Then we really got the bug and decided to get this. We do all our traveling in it. The smaller planes aren't possible with a family or for long trips, so this has been well worth it." He was starting the motor now. "Say"—he turned to Mr. Lowell—"if you would be good enough to pull the anchor—it's that crank on the side wall behind me—I won't have to bother my wife. She's a good crew but she's being guide for the rest of them."

While Daddy helped Mr. Hunter, Maggie, Carol and Mrs. Lowell were watching every step and listening hard as Mrs. Hunter fixed their safety belts. "We use these kapok life preservers as belts," she explained. "Not that we have ever needed them, but it's like keeping fire extinguishers in your house. Better be safe than sorry."

Mr. Hunter had the motor going very fast now. He checked all his instruments and then turned around from the pilot's seat high above the others on a sort of platform. "All set?" he asked.

"Take off," both Val and her mother called to him above the roar of the motor, as they must have many times before, from the natural way they said it.

Maggie gripped both arms of her chair and raised herself as far as the safety belt would let her, to be able to see better. She saw the pontoons cut through the water like skis, and a moment later they were up! Over the water! Steadily and smoothly, the plane climbed higher over the lake and as they approached the other side, turned and circled back over camp. Only then could Maggie turn to see how Mommy, Daddy and the others were liking it. She could hardly contain her unbounded joy. She could see from their faces they were enjoying it too and then she turned back to watch. There was camp! How tiny it looked way down there. The tennis courts looked so small! The canoes were like little paper boats you float in a bathtub. And she supposed those dots she could see were people, her friends at camp.

"I asked Daddy to fly over the course of your trip," Val called. "You'll be able to see just where you went. But it will be quick, so watch carefully." Mrs. Hunter unbuckled Maggie and said she could point out the way to Mr. Hunter. It wasn't easy to find from the air because it did look different, but Maggie was quick to get her bearings.

"There!" She pointed to a spot at the end of their lake. "There's the carry, along that little line that's the road. We went right through there to Big Rockwood. "That's that big lake." She had to smile to herself. It didn't look so big from the air. She remembered how on the trip she thought it was as big as an ocean.

"We had lunch on the shore just behind that point, and up farther is where we slept, where we found the lean-to." Mr. Hunter was flying lower now so they could get a good look.

"That's the spot!" Carol shrieked. "Where those boats are. Those people must have found our camping place! Didn't we have fun? But this is fun too," she added quickly. For she wanted them all to know what a good time she was having.

"Now let's head for the ocean, Jack," Mrs. Hunter said. "By the time we get to Bar Harbor, get anchored and ashore it will be late."

"Right," he responded, turning the plane about, climbing high into the sky again. In what seemed like no time at all, but was really forty minutes, they were over the ocean, readying to land in the harbor. Mr. Hunter circled about to give them all a fair chance at the view of the little town nestled along the shore, with the wide expanse of Atlantic beyond. For a moment Maggie hated to land. She wished they might fly on and on.

By the time they had finished a wonderful seafood dinner and had a walk around Bar Harbor Maggie and Carol felt like veteran fliers. Maggie looked forward to getting aboard again. "I never dreamed of anything like this," she told the Hunters in a grateful tone. "So much has happened I have to pinch myself to see if it's really me. And right now I'm not sure whether it's me or all a dream."

They all laughed and Mr. Hunter patted her head. "That's why we like to send Valerie here," he commented. "Because she meets so many nice girls from so many nice places. Sometime," he was talking to Mr. and Mrs. Lowell, "you must let Maggie come to New York and visit us."

"Could I? Would you let me?" she blurted out quickly.

"It could be," Mommy said.

"Fine," Mrs. Hunter added. "We'll arrange it for some vacation."

This time as Mr. Hunter warmed up the motor Maggie knew just what to expect. She watched the great pontoons as the plane started to move. This time the ocean waves made bumps as they skimmed along and then when the bumping stopped she knew they were up again. It seemed they had hardly been in the air at all before they were landing again at Sunset Lake. Val had to say good-bye to her mother and father right there in the plane for they were taking off again for New York.

"Good-bye, all," Mrs. Hunter said. "Write, dear," she added for Val's benefit.

The Hunters waited in the plane until the row-boat was back in the swimming area and then as the girls waved frantically the plane turned about and started off through the water. Like a giant bird it skimmed the surface and took off in flight. Mr. Hunter flew low, dipped a wing, and then the great bird headed south, back to the city again. They watched until it was out of sight, feeling sad. They were sorry to see the Hunters leave, for it meant the others would have to go soon.

Maggie gripped both Mommy's and Daddy's arms tightly. She hadn't said a word yet about going home with them. She had been sure before they got here that she would leave when they did but she hadn't mentioned it yet. Seeing the Hunters leave made her wonder again. Would she want to stay when her own parents left? Would she be happy or would she be miserable and lonesome again?

Yet in her heart, she knew. It was all right now. She would stay. She didn't feel so alone any more. She had begun to understand and like the other girls. She felt that she had friends here now—Carol and Val and Julie. Maggie liked Bobbie too. She was sorry she and Julie hadn't been with them today but maybe next year they'd have another chance.

Chapter Seven

Walking back to the bunk after saying good-
bye to her parents Maggie was not quite so sure. Maybe she had made a mistake, maybe she should have
gone with them, she thought, as she ambled along,
chin down, her spirits low. She was awfully glad to see
everyone when she walked into the bunk. They were
all sitting on Abbey's and Carol's beds.

"C'mon, Maggie," Carol said to her. "We've been
waiting for you. We thought we'd have a bull session."

"You all look as though you'd had a good time, a
nice week end," Abbey started. "How was your trip to
Bar Harbor?"

"Even I had a good time," Carol spoke up. "I didn't
expect to either. I thought it would be awful because
my parents were the only ones that weren't here. But

Maggie's mother and father were super. Wasn't I lucky . . ."

"You know," Maggie interrupted her, speaking without stopping to think, finding it easy this time to say just what was on her mind, "I thought when my parents left I would go with them. The first few weeks I was here I just hated it and I didn't think I'd be able to stay in camp until they came. I didn't know any of you and you didn't know me and I thought it was hopeless. Well, then I decided to stick it out till my parents came. But you know what," she looked up at them now, "I never even mentioned it to them when they were here. Now I feel better. I'm not so lonesome and I'm willing to stay."

The girls all looked at Maggie in amazement. Somehow they had gotten so used to her, they considered her so much a part of the picture at camp that they could hardly believe what she was saying.

"Why, Maggie," Val said. "We'd miss you terribly."

"I didn't know you felt as strongly as that," Carol said. "I guess I knew you were homesick now and then, like that time you stayed in the bunk all morning. But that happens to all of us once in a while. Did you know she felt that way?" Carol asked the others.

"Well, I did," Abbey spoke up when none of the others did. "And so did Paulie and your mother and father knew it too," Abbey told her and it was Maggie's turn to be amazed.

"Yes," Abbey went on. "They wrote me a letter and said they thought you were quite homesick and asked me what we could do to help."

Maggie looked at her thoughtfully and then asked, "And what did you do?"

"We made a point of helping you to do lots of things

we knew you liked and hoped that would make you feel better."

Maggie had to laugh in spite of herself. "It sure did!" she exclaimed. "I'm still here! And now I like it."

"We're all glad about that," Val stated with a ring of conviction. "What I like so much about you, Maggie, is that we can always count on you. No nonsense about you. We all know just where and just what with you. You say what you mean or you say nothing, as simple as that."

"And she's not bossy or superior like some people I know," Julie added, looking at Beth. But Beth remained silent. "After all, Maggie's a white cap and she'll make crew, and still she doesn't make us feel we're not good enough for her."

"Yes, and now that we know her she's a pack of fun too," Carol added.

Maggie listened to all this praise and admiration in utter disbelief. How can these girls who have so much feel this way about just plain me, she wondered. In all her life it had never occurred to her before to think about what she was like or what she had. She had been too busy with her few friends, her school and her home. She had known her place in the village where she had been born and had grown up, and she had never dreamed of any other kind of life for herself.

These girls, her new friends, lived in big cities, went to private schools, had been places and done things she had never thought about. She looked from one to the other, still finding it hard to believe, but she was pleased just the same. She could think of nothing to say, and yet here they were, making her feel she was part of them, telling her how much they liked her. In spite of all their differences they were friends, having fun together.

"You've all been a big help," she said gratefully. "Just remember, I wouldn't have had the plane ride or learned to swim so well or had that swell trip to Big Rockwood if I hadn't known all of you."

"All right," Abbey spoke up now. "We have something else to look forward to. We have our bunk trip to plan. Not that I want you to think I'm taking credit away from Maggie. She's done a good job here, and she deserves to be proud of herself. But there are three more weeks of camp and we want to get the most out of it."

"Mount Katahdin!" Julie popped out. "The kids who did that last year had a wonderful time."

"Why not an overnight canoe trip?" Maggie asked. "The same one we took last week unless someone has a better place."

After discussion Maggie was outvoted. The other girls preferred the trip to the highest mountain in the state of Maine. Maggie was disappointed it was not a water trip but she looked forward to it anyway. If all the others wanted it so much it must be fun, she realized.

"Well, thank goodness," Beth said when it was definitely decided. "I thought after all that goo you would do whatever Maggie wanted. Do you know what's on my mind?" She made it sound important. "My father told me if I win any of the awards for being best in camp he'll get me my own horse. I don't know what to try for. What do you think I could get best in camp for, Abbey?"

"You certainly are a talented girl, Beth. But I'd hate to say where to put all your energy because I might pick the wrong thing," Abbey answered. "Have you yourself any preferences?"

"Well, if I thought I could win the diving—I really love that. Is there an award for that?" she asked.

"Sure," Julie reminded her. "Don't you remember Ann Mason got it last year? And you got mention as the third best. Wasn't that girl from Boston, who didn't come back, second?"

"Mm," Beth nodded. "And I'd still have to be better than Ann . . ."

"Gee, isn't that exciting, to think of having your own horse to ride whenever you want," Carol said.

"Well, I have to win first," Beth explained. "You don't know my father."

"You do lots of things well," Val spoke up. "But we'd all like you lots better if you weren't so darned snippy. Why don't you try to match your disposition to the rest of you?"

"Yes," Abbey took it up there. "If you did, you would be in the running for the best camper cup." Abbey let that sink in a moment and then went on. "That's the root of your trouble, Beth. Everyone admires your ability, but few girls like you. We'd do what we could to help you get your horse if you would do your part, be a little humble, a little less superior."

"O.K. It's time to pounce on me," Julie spoke up. "Come on and tear me apart now, you vultures." She laughed as she said it, but you could tell she expected to be gone at with hammer and tongs.

"Julie." It was Carol who started in on her. "You're a good kid but you don't give yourself half a chance. You're scared and worried about something all the time. What's eating you anyway?"

Before Julie could say a word Val took it up. "But

you have to know Julie better and then you'll understand."

"Well, why is it that no one really knows her except you?" Carol asked. "After all we've bunked together for two years. Yet I feel Julie is with us about half the time. The rest of it she seems off by herself in a daze."

"Maybe you're being a little smug now," Beth put in. "You think everybody has to be like yourself. Maybe you kids don't like me because you're jealous of me. Well, I want to be the best swimmer, rider, dancer—it's worth it to me. That's what my father and mother have taught me. Val maybe could get her own horse no matter what she does but I'll get my horse only if I win it. It's like a prize. I was allowed to come to camp as a prize too, for being at the head of my class. If nobody cared what I did I'd be more like Julie. That's the trouble with her. She doesn't know whether her parents care—like on Visitors Day. She didn't know till a day or so before if both her parents would come. Do you think that makes her feel good?"

Julie looked up with a startled expression. Beth was saying things that clicked with her. "Beth is partly right," she was surprised to hear herself say. "I want to have fun with you all but sometimes I just can't. When Carol's mother and father don't come on Visitors Day she knows why. It's perfectly simple, but with my parents I don't know why and I never know what to expect. Bobbie and I don't know right now whether we're going back to the house or not. My mother writes she'd like to get an apartment in the city, or else let my father take us for the winter. She says a house is too much for her by herself. I asked my daddy if that would be all right with him. He said it would be but he didn't ask us to please come with him. Sort of 'if no one else takes you I will.'" Julie's eyes were filled with tears now. She couldn't say any more and the girls felt badly for her. Julie had said things she had never thought of before. They had just tumbled out. Having said them she began to examine these thoughts.

"My best friend in Washington has the same trouble," Beth told them. "But now she's gotten used to it and she likes being away from her family better than with them. She goes to my school, and sometimes she doesn't even go home for vacations. She has her own friends and that's what counts."

"Well, Julie, you can count on us as your friends," Maggie comforted her. "And maybe that will help."

Julie nodded gratefully.

"You know," Val was talking now. "I can never count on my parents for the ordinary things. When it comes to a birthday or Christmas or some special occasion they're wonderful. But half the time they're away or so busy with their own affairs that I don't see them, and sometimes I feel I don't even know what they're like."

"But your parents always come through in a pinch," Julie said.

"Yes, it's in the other things that I miss them. Parents like Maggie's mother and father are what I dream of having. It's worth more having parents like that than all the money in the world. Sometimes I feel like the poor little rich girl. Who was it said the Lowells were like friends? Well, my parents take care of me but they're not my friends."

"It's not easy to know how to make friends of your children," Abbey put in. "Taking care of them and loving them is the first job. If a parent can do more than that it's so much gravy. My parents weren't able to be my friends either but they were very nice parents. They worked hard to take care of me and my sisters and brother. The rest of it was up to me. I made my own friends."

The bull session shifted to Carol then. "She talks too much," Beth said. It was her chance to get back at Carol for all the digs she had made. "She always has to put her two cents' worth into everything. Otherwise she's not a bad egg."

"That seems fair enough to me," Julie agreed. "She's fun and full of the dickens all the time, but she does talk too much sometimes. Just put a harness on her tongue and she'll be all set."

"Before we get the harness on," Carol spoke up, "let's do a job on Val. We haven't gotten to her yet."

"No, and I want to say right here and now," Julie interrupted, "that Val is a wonderful friend. She's generous and thoughtful and that's a lot."

"I can't understand about you, Val," Maggie remarked. "How grown-up you are. It isn't only that you have evening dresses and things like that. But you think and say things the rest of us don't know yet."

"Sometimes she's too darn grown-up if you ask me," Beth said. "Not that you're bigger or smarter than us," she tried to explain what she meant to Val. "But it's like this bull session. You've said things about all of us and about your own parents that sound like a report card from school, like what a teacher would say, or Abbey."

"Why not put it," Abbey suggested, "that some girls excel at sports, and some make fine friends and some understand people, and everyone can't be everything."

Maggie was busy trying to absorb all she had heard, as Abbey went on.

"You don't seem to mind hurting each other's feelings too much. You certainly do know what you think of each other and you have actually been pretty straight in pointing out each other's weaknesses. If it helps us to have a better time, to enjoy and understand each other better, then this kind of a session is worthwhile."

Slowly they began to get ready for bed. There was a warmth, a close friendly feeling that had not existed before. Maggie supposed it was because they knew what was bothering each other, because they had had a glimpse of the problems in back of each girl. Maggie realized that the other girls actually envied her because of her parents. Somehow she felt that Beth had been even more envious of her parents than Val. Were Beth's parents like that all the time, she wondered, always asking a price for anything they gave? She wouldn't like that, Maggie decided. It made what you could do more important than anything, and if you couldn't do a thing, why you were just no good. No wonder Beth always needed to be the only one or the best one or the first one. It isn't that Beth doesn't like me, Maggie concluded. She's just jealous because I got a white cap too.

As Maggie was falling asleep she couldn't help smiling to herself to think how differently she had felt just a few short weeks ago. Only three more weeks of camp —and she was actually worried to think she might not get a chance to do all the things she wanted! If they went on the Mt. Katahdin trip would she have time to go on another canoe trip?

Each bunk at Sunset Lake Camp was allowed one day, during the last few weeks of camp, when the girls could do whatever they chose. They usually voted for trips away from camp, either in the station wagon, by canoe, or, in the case of the younger girls, by motor launch. In the next few days Maggie heard what each bunk was planning. One of the senior bunks was going to visit another camp for a day. One bunk was going on a long drive over to New Hampshire to see Mt. Washington and the Presidential Range as well as some of the famous winter sports places.

"But they're not going to climb a mountain themselves," Carol commented.

The senior Bunk One had persuaded Miss Wright and Mickey Fisher, the dramatic counselor, to drive down to Skowhegan for the famous summer theater there. But Maggie and the girls of her bunk weren't jealous of that. They were busy planning their day of mountain climbing.

On the morning of their trip they got up quietly at six o'clock, had breakfast and were already piling into the station wagon just as the bugle blew for the rest of the camp to get up. It was a merry crew that started off, singing away at the top of their lungs. They sang all the while they bumped over the dirt roads on the long drive to the base of the mountain.

The scenery was beautiful as they sped along through sparsely settled country, stretches of woods sprinkled with lakes and ponds, across little wooden bridges over rivers and streams. Then Victor, who drove the camp car, said to them, "There she is, your mountain, dead ahead."

Maggie craned her neck to get a good view. They were all ecstatic as they approached. This was going to be quite an event, to climb that great high mountain that seemed to grow taller as they drew nearer to the base.

When the car stopped they were surprised to find a public camp site with a few stores and a good many people. Everyone was very friendly as they took a good look around. Maggie was impatient to start climbing. "C'mon, let's go," she urged the others. They had determined in advance to get to the top and now that they had seen Mt. Katahdin in all its splendor they knew it would not be easy. It was much higher than any of the mountains around camp.

The trail was wide at the base and they started up at a fast pace. But after a short while the path grew narrower, more winding and steeper. They proceeded in single file then and it wasn't long before the canteens and the lunch boxes seemed weighted with lead.

They came across a group of boys sitting around on some rocks and Abbey said, "Let's rest here awhile too. I think we'll do better if we stop for a bit."

"Plenty of room here, and it's nice and shady," one of the boys spoke up. "We've had our rest. What camp are you from?"

Beth answered, and then asked them, "And where are you from?"

"We're from the Rangeley Lakes, Camp Kennebago. We've been out a week already . . ."

"You mean away from camp?" Val asked as she realized the packs on their backs were blanket rolls and that they must have been camping out all that time. "How did you do it?"

Maggie crowded in close to listen as the boys told how they hiked and camped. She couldn't help but feel envious of all their adventures. This was the end of their trip. They were going to the top where they would camp for the night, and then tomorrow when they came down they would telephone for their camp truck to pick them up.

"Gee, I wish we could do that," Julie said. "That sounds even better. Do you think we could?" Maggie was glad to know that someone else felt the way she did.

"We're not prepared this time," Abbey told her and then went on to explain to the boys. "We're on our bunk trip. We left camp early this morning and we'll be back there tonight. We hope to reach the top before three so we'd better be on our way soon."

In a few minutes, the boys started off. "So long and good luck," they waved. "Maybe we'll see you again. We're not in a hurry."

The girls got under way again soon after the boys. They could hear them up ahead. They hoped to catch up to them but after another stiff ascent they stopped again in a small clearing. "Look at the view from here," Maggie exclaimed, and they all turned to admire the broad vista of mountains and valleys spread out before them. They were level with the tops of some of the surrounding mountains and would soon be higher than anything else around. "Let's make one more sally before we stop for lunch," Maggie suggested.

Just as they were picking up their things, the penetrating wail of a siren made them all stand still as statues. What a strange sound that was here, its ominous tone breaking the stillness! Fire! There must be a forest fire! Immediately they were alert, scanning the horizon, watching for smoke. They looked at each other, not knowing what to think or do next. Just then the boys and their counselor hurried down the trail.

Maggie was speechless as she heard Abbey ask, "What's up? What should we do?"

"Don't know yet," the boys' counselor answered. "We may have to go down to find out." And as the siren blew again, a long terrible wail, he said, "The siren is definitely above us. I think we should stay right here until we find out. Someone is bound to come down. . . ."

Before he could finish a young man raced down the path. Dressed in shorts and regulation camp clothes, he didn't look like a forester. "A child is lost! Eight kids and two counselors camped for the night at the shelter just above here and one of them is missing. They just discovered it. They thought she had gone ahead to the top, but when they got there, there was no sign of her."

Soon he had told the whole story. The girl was ten years old. She hadn't been seen since the night before. Her things were all with the others, but there was no sign of her. "Did you see anyone on your way up?" the young man asked. "Her group is just about hysterical. We'll all have to help. The kid may have fallen and been hurt."

Maggie looked about with a different feeling. Someone could easily fall from many places on the trail, she realized. If you were hurt you might lie there for —Maggie couldn't think about it any more. It was too scary. But what an awful thing! However did it happen, she wondered.

"How far up is the shelter where they camped?" Abbey asked.

"It's at four thousand feet, not too far from the top. About a half hour climb from here," the man answered. "I'm with a Scout troop from Bangor and we were at the top last night. That's how we heard about it—when a counselor and one of the girls came to look for her."

The boys' counselor interrupted to ask, "How many people are above us, besides her group?"

"There are twelve of us, and there's her group, nine now, and a forester."

Maggie did some quick arithmetic, twelve and nine and the six of them, and the forester. Hardly enough people to search the whole mountain.

"Well I think we ought to fan out as far as we can and then at a signal call her name. What is her name?" the counselor asked.

"Mary, Mary Hiscock. They've been calling down from the top. Haven't you heard them?"

"We heard nothing until the siren," Abbey answered. "But that's a good idea. Let's fan out and work our way up. Then if we don't find her, we'll try it coming down. You lead us," Abbey said to the other counselor. "And by the way, what's your name? I'm Abbey Wittmer."

"Sorry." He managed a smile in the face of everyone's fear. "I'm Keith Butler. Glad to meet you, Abbey. The others can introduce themselves. No time for formalities now."

He spoke to all of them. "We're going to spread out as far as we can, keeping within reach of the person on either side. That way we'll have no mishaps. I'll stay in the center, the two counselors take either end. We'll all call together—Mary, Mary Hiscock! Keep your voices as low-pitched as possible, they carry better that way."

The boys and girls were quick to carry out the commands, eager to do all they could. They spread out as directed till those on either end were out of the clearing altogether and in heavy undergrowth. It was hard to get a footing and even harder to hold it. Maggie had wondered why they had to stay so close, but now she understood. Then a signal from Keith and they yelled, with all the voice they could muster.

"Mary, Mary Hiscock!" went up the cry. It seemed to Maggie that anyone on the next mountain should be able to hear them. As they stood quietly, silent and attentive, they heard only the echo, "Mary, Mary Hiscock," coming back to them. Then the silence settled thickly again as they waited vainly for an answer.

Surely anyone above would hear that. The one slim hope they had was that perhaps they couldn't hear Mary Hiscock's reply. Or suppose she was hurt and couldn't call out? She might even be unconscious. At a signal from Keith they tried again, even louder this time. And they waited longer to hear an answer. But only the same echo and the same heavy silence came back. Maggie was really worried—what would they do now? As though answering her thought, they inched their way along the side of the mountain at Keith's suggestion to try from another point. It was almost impossible to find a footing once they were off the trail, but they went on anyhow, with a feeling of urgency.

"I hear something," one of the boys shouted. "Quiet, everyone!" The response was immediate. Hardly a twig crackled.

"That's from below," Keith said after listening intently. "Someone's coming up. I hope there are a lot of people so we can circle the whole mountain." In a few minutes people streamed into the clearing, breathless from the rapid climb. They took places at the ends of the line. They didn't need to be told what to do, they could see this was a grim business and they had come to help. Some carried axes which they dropped now, knowing it was not fire they had to fight.

People kept coming up steadily, Maggie noticed, as she caught a glimpse of the trail below. First it had been men and big boys, now women and children were puffing along. The story went down the line. Girl lost! Mary Hiscock. And when they had all spread out again Maggie couldn't see the end of the line in either direction. They would surely get Mary this way. She hoped it would be soon because the girl must be frightened to pieces, lost for so long. How long they didn't even know.

Maggie had to pay careful attention now. She was no longer near the trail and it wasn't easy to get a footing. The trees were thick and close and the ground seemed to run straight up and down. Between her concern for Mary Hiscock and trying to keep herself from falling she was having a hard time of it. As she looked around she shivered when she saw how easy it would be to topple over, get caught in the brush, or by a rock. Maybe Mary Hiscock couldn't answer, maybe she was dead already. The thought was too awful. Maggie stayed close to the boys on either side of her.

Then like an electric current passing through wire the word came down the line. Mary had been found! Every face mirrored the concern that all of them felt. Was she all right? Was she alive? What had happened? They began inching back to the clearing again, everyone talking in low voices. Maggie was really frightened now. Something awful must have happened. Word spread along. Mary had been hurt. They had found her near the path. She was alive. She was unconscious. The rumors spread fast. Maggie didn't know what to believe.

Back at the clearing again she looked around for Abbey and her bunk mates. It was a relief to be together again.

"Oh, Abbey," Julie sighed. "Thank goodness we're all here. What happened? Did you see her?"

"She's all right. She wasn't really hurt!" Abbey had gotten the story straight from Keith. Nothing else seemed to matter for a moment, they were all so relieved there was no tragedy. "But what happened to her?" Val wanted to know.

"She had to get up during the night. When she started back to her camp site she went in the wrong direction. And it took only a few minutes for her to realize she was lost. She called out but no one heard her. Either she was already too far away or they were too fast asleep. In a panic, she tried to run, took a spill and turned her ankle. She crawled along on her hands and knees after that, looking for a place to wait for morning. And every inch she went carried her farther from the camp site although she thought she had changed her direction. When she came to a level place big enough to stretch out, she covered herself with dry leaves and waited. That was a wise and sensible thing for her to do. But by then she was too scared to fall asleep.

"From her face it looked as though she had been crying for days although Keith thinks she got lots of insect bites and they made her face swell up. Anyway by the time it was light and also somewhat warmer she was exhausted and did fall asleep. She didn't wake up until she heard the siren. That scared her again because she thought she would be caught in a forest fire. Not until she heard the yells did she realize the siren was for her. She called as loud as she could for at least a half hour before we heard her. Anyway she's safe—frightened, hungry and dirty, but except for a swollen ankle and a puffed-up face she's all right."

"Oh," Julie let out a deep groan. "I would have died if that had happened to me. Thank goodness it wasn't any of us."

Beth had been near where they had found Mary. "You should have seen her counselor," she told them now. "She was almost crazy and when they heard Mary's voice she fell into a heap and couldn't even walk to where Mary was. They had to help Mary get to her. It was awful."

"Well," Abbey explained. "She must have been frantic. Think how I would feel if anything happened to any of you."

They stayed together, their own little group, talking it over in detail—how frightened they were, what each of them would have done had she been lost. And before they knew it, it was two o'clock. "We haven't had lunch yet! Let's eat!"

They perched on rocks at the edge of the path, and took out their lunches. Beth, Val and Carol were famished but Julie and Maggie couldn't eat. "I guess Mary Hiscock stole my appetite." Maggie smiled feebly. She couldn't make herself eat. She did take a drink of water from her canteen and then offered her sandwiches to the others. Julie felt the same way as Maggie.

"When I'm excited," she told them, "I just can't manage to chew. It's as though the food were nails. If I force myself it doesn't work either 'cause it goes down to my tummy and feels like rocks."

"What are we going to do now?" Carol wanted to

know. Somehow finishing their climb with the same gay happy feeling as before didn't seem possible.

Abbey looked at all their faces and then suggested, "Maybe we should go down the mountain now. We can ask Victor to take us for a ride before we go back to camp. I think we've had enough excitement for one day."

They didn't even need to discuss it. To go up the trail no longer had the same appeal. "Anyway we did have an adventure," Julie said. "We can't say we didn't have a big time."

"You said it," Val added. "And thank goodness it had a happy ending. I wonder if that girl will ever want to go mountain climbing again. I think I'll stick to canoes when we have our bunk trip next year."

The reception the girls of Bunk Five got when they arrived back at camp was not what they had anticipated. They were surprised to see Miss Wright at the gate waiting for them. She looked them all over carefully as they got out of the car.

"It came over the radio," she explained. "We knew the girl had been found, and we knew it wasn't one of you. But the radio did say there were several sprained ankles and wrists among the rescuers and we were very worried about you."

They all proudly held out their arms and pranced on their feet to show they were safe and sound. Then Miss Wright invited them into the counselors' sitting room. "I'd like to give you a chance to tell us about it. But there is no point in upsetting the younger children by talking all over camp. They don't know anything about it."

Miss Wright and Brownie and Miss Strang were all there to hear the story. The girls told about meeting the boys' camp group, the siren, the Boy Scout leader who told them what happened, how they fanned out around the mountain, how scary it was. They spared no details. "I don't think there ever were so many people up on Mt. Katahdin at one time before. It was really crowded. And Keith Butler and the search party did a wonderful job."

"How long did it take us to find her?" Beth asked. "About an hour?"

"The siren blew at twenty after ten," Abbey said. "And Mary was found at ten after twelve. Glad it didn't seem any longer to you," she added. "I thought it was an eternity."

"And I didn't have any lunch," Julie spoke up. "The rest of you had something to eat, but Maggie and I didn't and I'm starving."

"We'll have something in a moment," Miss Wright was saying. "I just ordered some sandwiches and tea and cake for you."

Chapter Eight

FROM THAT TIME UNTILL THE END OF THE SEASON, camp was better than Maggie had counted on. Somehow after their big adventure everything they did together was more fun and more cherished. They worked well and had fun doing it. Maggie went down for crew practice every afternoon. Being on a team with seven other girls, learning all that crew meant—racing forms, distance strokes—was wonderful fun.

Even Beth's jealousy and need to climb over everyone didn't matter as much. Maggie had managed to keep her distance and Beth seemed to leave her alone these days—until the day Maggie was given a chance to paddle bow in the war canoe. Beth was in the other canoe and as they came off the water Paulie called them all to the paddle house.

"Today we're going to break up into small teams to get ready for regular canoe racing. We'll have eight canoes and that ought to make a pretty good race. I think you will have fun and each of you will be able to paddle either bow or stern. If you have any choices speak up now."

The seniors paired off easily. They made up four boats right away. Then it was up to Paulie to assign the others. "What about you two?" She pointed to Beth and Maggie. "How about Beth taking stern and Maggie bow?"

Maggie didn't know what to do when she heard Beth say, "Why do I have to be with Maggie? Can't I stern for a stronger girl?"

"You could," Paulie answered her evenly and sweetly. "But more important than your paddling is your team work. You'd better work on that for a while."

Beth was a good stern paddler, Maggie knew, and so she was willing to make the best of it. Maybe, she thought, Beth would be friendlier when they were forced to paddle together. She soon realized, however, that it would have been better if they had not been assigned to each other.

The next day when they started practicing in the small canoes Maggie had a hard time. No matter what she did Beth would criticize her. "Take a longer stroke," she would say impatiently. Or, "Can't you pull harder?" with exasperation in her voice.

Maggie listened to her until she had all she could take. She was doing her best, working hard. It wasn't just the criticism she minded but the unpleasant tone of Beth's voice, as though she were doing the wrong thing on purpose. Finally she deliberately set her paddle across the gunwales and turned around to face Beth.

"Look," she said, stirred to anger, her eyes flashing. "I didn't choose you for a partner either. You're not the best paddler in camp so don't try to blame me if you don't get your horse. And besides, Paulie is the coach of canoeing in this camp and not you."

Beth's eyes changed to a cold nasty expression; her mouth drew in to a firm straight line. Maggie was almost frightened—she had never seen Beth look this angry before. Beth couldn't admit to herself that she wasn't the best paddler in camp so it was intolerable for someone like Maggie to say it. With Maggie still facing her she picked up her paddle and headed toward shore. Maggie just sat there, waiting to see what she would do, expecting to be dumped at any moment. But what Beth did do was even more surprising.

"Miss Paul," Beth called in a formal cold voice. "I don't think I want to go out for crew. I'd rather spend the time at the diving board. This won't work out for me anyway. I'd like to report to Brownie now. . . ."

"Beth, what made you change all of a sudden? How come you didn't say that when you were assigned yesterday?"

"I didn't have a chance to think about it. But I really want to get ready for the diving. I'd like to be excused now. . . ." She was getting up, ready to get out of the canoe.

Paulie looked from one to the other. Maggie sat as still as a mouse. She wasn't going to say a word. "Tell you what," Paulie said to Beth. "You stick it out this week and I'll see what I can work out. I still think you need to work with someone. You do everything else on your own, Beth, diving, swimming, piano, riding. Team work would be a good thing for you, so let's see how it goes. You'll have time for your diving in the morning."

Beth was so angry she had to bite her lips. She hadn't expected Paulie to see through her plan, and she couldn't even look at her now. When Maggie spoke up she didn't seem to hear her. "Maybe it would be better then," Maggie was saying, "if Beth could be assigned to someone else. She doesn't like me. . . ."

"Oh, Maggie, you're mistaken, I'm sure. Why, of course Beth likes you," Paulie smiled at her. "You're an excellent bow paddler. Now you both get out there and work hard."

Reluctantly they paddled back out. They were both so perturbed they paddled in a crazy fashion. First one would let the paddle slide through the water with no push behind it. Then the next stroke would be hard and angry to make up for it. They just sat in the canoe and went through the motions. They listened to Paulie's coaching and soon Maggie grew interested in working on her strokes. She wondered how Beth felt but she was determined not to ask or even turn around to see.

"I'd like to paddle starboard," Maggie gathered her courage to say. "Let's switch."

Beth didn't answer but Maggie could tell from the slight lurch of the canoe that she had picked up her paddle and changed sides. "O.K." Beth called out. "Give it all you have," she couldn't resist adding.

At the end of practice Beth and Maggie parted abruptly and Maggie didn't see her again till bedtime. Then Beth came up to her. "Don't you think Paulie would pay more attention to you? Why don't you see if you can get us out of this? I really do need the time for diving practice. I want that horse, you know."

"Gee, Beth." Maggie looked at her with pity. "She would know it was a put-up job. Maybe she'll let you go the last week."

It was a struggle for Beth to accept that but she had no choice unless she played sick, and then she'd have to stay out of everything. She had but one purpose and anything else was in her way, just a nuisance to her. Maggie couldn't help but feel sorry for her. It must be awful to be that way.

For the rest of the week when they went down for practice Beth seemed more willing to put up with her fate, but Maggie knew it was only in order to be released. Crew could have been so much fun if Maggie had had a partner who enjoyed it, who would laugh with her, who would talk it all over in an easy, relaxed way. She still had fun in the war canoe which took the first part of every afternoon and she consoled herself with the thought that the two-crew work helped her to do better in the war canoe.

At the last practice of the week Paulie called Beth and Maggie over. "Suppose I reassign you girls. Your week is up. Maggie, you go with Nancy. Try paddling stern today. And Beth, you paddle with Ethel and take bow."

Maggie was thrilled to get a chance to paddle stern and she worked hard at it all afternoon. She wondered how Beth was feeling, for Paulie hadn't let her change over to diving. At the end of practice Maggie was surprised when Beth called, "Hey, Maggie, how did you like stern this afternoon?"

"I liked it fine, but I'm not very good at it." She hadn't expected Beth to be interested in anything she did. "How about you?" she asked politely.

"Well, it was all right," Beth was toeing the sand, looking down as she spoke. "But you and I were getting along better. I'd just as soon stick it out with you if you're willing."

Quick as a flash Maggie came back at her. "Sure, if we half tried working together we'd probably win a place." The two of them hurried over to Paulie, and Maggie stood back, giving Beth a chance to talk.

"I'd just as soon stick it out with Maggie till the end," Beth said, "if it's all right with you, Paulie."

Paulie couldn't conceal her pleasure. "Why, that's fine. What made you change your mind, Beth?"

"Well, we got used to each other this week. It was better at stern with Maggie than at bow with Ethel. . . ."

"Mm. I see," Paulie said. "Well, all right. You can team up again."

This was the last week of camp. Regular camp activities were abandoned to give each girl the chance to do the things she wanted the most. There was a lot to do and everyone was busy every second. Bunk Five was coaxing Julie to take her white cap test.

"You can do it," they teased, and got Brownie to sign her up. The whole bunk went down to cheer her on, to encourage her. When Julie came out of the water after her long swim—the thing she had been most frightened of—she told them, "I never would have made it if you hadn't been there. But when I saw you I just couldn't let you down." The grin was all over her face, she was so pleased with herself. The girls hugged her, wet though she was. Now every girl in Bunk Five was a white cap, except Carol, and she was as good as one.

The tennis matches were first on the schedule of

final events, and everyone turned out to see them. Watching tennis played well is a lovely sight. Maggie loved the applause that burst forth after every good shot, and the cheers when a match was won made her spine tingle. In the tennis matches you knew at once who won, you didn't have to wait till the final banquet to find out. But for the results in riding, dancing, and some of the other sports you had to wait until the end. The suspense on the night of the banquet was always intense.

Maggie entered lots of the water events. She was in form swimming for breast stroke and side stroke, on the intermediate relay team, and of course the crew. The crew events were to her the most important of all. She knew she wasn't in a class with the best swimmers, had no chance of winning those events, but she was hopeful that her war canoe might win. There were only two canoes and her whole team was very pepped up. They were all in position now, eight girls at attention, their paddles up and ready, waiting for the signal to start.

A shrill blast on the whistle. Stroke—together—stroke! They were off! The paddles all dipped simultaneously, each one of the eight girls in her canoe and in the other one too. They were paddling with all their might, out to win.

Maggie managed to glance at the next canoe. They were ahead—just two braces. But she wasn't discouraged. She just doubled her efforts and pulled the paddle through the water with all her strength.

"Stroke, together. Stroke," the words were drawn out to encourage the girls to take long hard pulls. Maggie saw they were drawing even with the other boat. The stroke in the bow must have seen it too for she went even faster now, increasing the pace.

"Stroke—hard—stroke—hard," she called to them, her voice rising.

There was the finish tape up ahead. Just a few more strokes. "Stroke and stroke and stroke," the bow called to them. "And finish! We won!" she yelled.

Maggie had seen the bow of her canoe cut across the tape first, the other canoe only a second behind them. All of them leaned back against the braces now, breathless, puffing, but smiling and content in victory.

Before they could congratulate each other the girls in the other canoe hailed them. "We don't see—how you did it—whew," the bow paddler in the other canoe called over. "You deserve to win. I don't think I could have paddled another two strokes."

The whole camp cheered them as they paddled in to shore. This time they went easily, barely pulling on the paddles, gliding in—the winners! And as they beached, they raised their paddles in salute, acknowledging the cheer of victory.

"While the paddlers are resting for the two-crew races, we'll have diving," Brownie announced. There were seven girls in the line. "There will be a standing front, a running front, a back dive and a jackknife. Then one optional dive."

There was Beth on the line right after Ann Mason. And Maggie noticed that Beth and Jean Barrett were the only two girls who weren't seniors. It would be hard for Beth to compete with those big girls, but she did hope for her sake and for the horse that she would win.

One after the other they did their dives, so many lovely, graceful and difficult performances. The rest of the camp, the spectators, were silent, even breathless as they watched. As far as Maggie could tell Beth was doing as well as any of them. Maggie hadn't paid much attention to diving this summer. Every once in a while she would go up on the board and dive off, but she had never gone in for coaching, learning fancy dives or good form. She found herself thinking, next summer I'll have to go in for diving, it looks like fun. Next summer! Would she be back here next summer? As she sat resting, waiting for the two-crew race, thinking about next summer, she laughed to herself. Well, she would see, she would think about it.

She and Beth were in their canoe now, paddling out to take their place at the starting point. "Gee, Beth, I sure hope you win. If I were the judge I'd give you first—you dive wonderfully. That last dive, where you did a somersault, what do you call that?"

"The one-and-a-half," Beth told her. "If I do win the diving it will be because of that. Ann Mason is better than I am at the others."

"Are you tired?" Maggie asked.

"No, are you? Diving isn't tiring. But you were in the war canoe, how about you? Your crew won."

"You know," Maggie said to her now, almost in a whisper. "I bet we could win this race. The others are all heavier than we are and that ought to make up for what we lack in strength. What do you say we try?"

"You know, Maggie, you're a good kid. I've been hard on you and I'm sorry. I don't want to be mean, that's just the way I am. If you want to try I'll try with you. Not for myself but because you want to."

Maggie couldn't say anything then. She just flashed a look of gratitude and pleasure at Beth, as they pulled into position, ready and eager to go. Maggie knew she would paddle even harder this time.

"Attention!"

"Paddles up!"

The whistle! They were off! This time they didn't have to yell stroke. Beth just watched Maggie and Maggie set the pace. She couldn't wait to get her paddle out of the water, to feather over and put it in again. Maggie worked so hard that she had no chance to look at the others. There was only one thing, the tape up front. She could feel Beth keeping the rhythm with her. Nearer and nearer, they paddled in perfect unison. The tape was still taut. Maggie practically stood up to make the stroke, to reach way forward with her paddle, to pull the boat ahead.

The tape! They cut it!

Maggie practically fell over the bow of the canoe. She lay there panting, unable to sit up or hold her paddle. She hadn't seen the other canoes, she didn't know what had happened.

"Maggie, you were wonderful," she heard Beth gasping behind her.

She picked herself up then. "What's the matter?" she asked as she turned about.

"We won!" Beth almost screamed at her. "We're the best crew in camp! And you did it. Look at the others. We not only won but we won by half a length."

Paulie paddled up to them. "The custom is to dump the winners. But I'm afraid you two are done in. This is Maggie's second big race and she's pretty tired. . . ."

"Oh, dump us then." Maggie was still panting. "We can take it, can't we, Beth?"

Paulie looked up sharply as she heard that. "Sure,

Maggie," Beth was saying. "Let's not miss any of the fun."

Beth and Maggie were the heroes of Bunk Five. The girls couldn't stop talking about their wonderful race. "Look." Julie held her hands up. "I bit off the rest of my nails. Just when they were beginning to grow. I never saw anything like the way you two went."

They were all astonished to hear Beth say, "Maggie did it. Give her the credit."

"No, Beth," Abbey spoke up then. "You both did it. I must say I was proud of you. I think everyone was. And you both deserve the credit."

Something had happened to Beth today. She sat quietly on her bed now, interested, part of the group, and yet she looked puzzled. She actually was trying to understand what had happened. It wasn't easy to figure out. She and Maggie had paddled a good race, they hadn't really expected to win. They had done it to please each other. That part of it was the most fun, the fun that no one else shared with them. Beth got up and went outside. In a minute she came back with the lovely white bathing suit and walked up to Maggie.

"Here, would you like this suit?" She held it out. "I feel like giving you something."

Maggie could only look at Beth. She knew how Beth loved that suit, how precious it was to her. She had saved it for special occasions all summer and had worn it today for the diving contest. Maggie didn't know what to say.

"Gee, Beth," she finally managed to stutter, still standing there, overwhelmed by the offer.

"You're a good kid, Maggie, and I'm sorry for everything. Now we can be friends." Beth was still holding out the cherished suit.

Maggie looked around at the other girls, wondering what she could say. "Oh, let's just be friends. All of us together. You keep the suit, Beth." Maggie was embarrassed. "I wouldn't have any place to wear it and it looks so well on you."

Five happier girls couldn't have been found anywhere that afternoon. They would stop to hug each other, to lend a hand, to admire one another. They planned round-robin letters for the winter and all talked about being together again next summer. As they finished their packing they made sure they had each and every home address safely tucked in their trunks.

They went to the final banquet with faces glowing, arms linked, and singing. They could hardly wait to hear about the awards, yet they already had a sense of accomplishment. A feeling of friendship and love spread through all of them and it was an achievement no one had to reward them for, or tell them about.

More than once that evening, as the awards were announced, all five of them were taken by surprise. They got the pennant for the best-kept bunk in camp. They and the senior Bunk One were the only two in camp to have all expert swimmers. Even though Carol couldn't dive she had the privileges of a white cap. Maggie and Beth got letters for crew. The others all got at least one letter each—Julie for dramatics, Val for horsemanship, and on down the line. Each mention that came to them brought cheers and squeals of delight from them all.

Then at the end came the awards for the best in camp. They all waited with bated breath. Would Beth win? Would she earn her horse? They sat quietly, hoping with her. As one after another name was mentioned, but not Beth's, the girls started to get nervous.

"Diving!" came Brownie's voice. Beth couldn't look up. Maggie couldn't breathe. "Ann Mason first! Beth Morgan second!" The other names didn't matter now. Maggie felt as though she would cry. Beth was biting her lips and fingering the salt shaker while she whispered, "It's all right. I sure would have liked my own horse. I guess my father will be disappointed in me. But I don't feel heart-broken. I'll get along."

Miss Wright was making the final speech now about the camp family, and the progress that had been made in the time they had been together. "There are some things for which we don't have awards, but I would like to mention them and congratulate you anyway. They are even more valuable accomplishments, or perhaps I should say goals, to strive for— signposts on your way." Bunk Five was hardly listening, they were so concerned with Beth. They were scarcely aware that Miss Wright was talking. But all of a sudden their ears perked up.

"The girls in Bunk Five, for example," Miss Wright went on. "They had the best-kept bunk in camp but they did much more than that. They worked out some serious problems together and every one of them deserves credit. Every single girl in that bunk has learned to live more happily than before she came to camp." They sat up straight and proud when this reached them. There were knowing looks flashed from one to another as Miss Wright said, "I think they deserve a cheer and maybe we'll work out a new award on that basis."

The evening ended with the whole camp singing together. Though there had been some disappointments, there were funny things too that helped make up for them. Paulie came up to Maggie when they started back to their bunks. "Tell me, Maggie, how are the girls? Did you make any friends? Do you remember that we have a date to talk at the end of camp?"

"Oh, Paulie," Maggie giggled. "I've had a wonderful time. I want to come back next year too. Do you know what?" she confided. "I really hate to leave."

"Well, that's interesting, coming from you." Paulie smiled. "It was worth it then, to wait, and be patient. And do you know what?" She borrowed the phrase from Maggie. "Next summer I expect you to win one of those cups. Just in case you are interested your name was mentioned as a possibility this year. All the counselors think you are a fine all-round camper."

Those words put Maggie in a trance. Was Paulie trying to make her feel good? As she thought about it she knew that Paulie wasn't like that, she wouldn't say something she didn't mean. It was more than Maggie could believe, however.

Getting ready for bed each of the girls was lost in her thoughts, until Beth spoke up. "You know," she said. "This has been my best summer at camp—even if I didn't earn the horse. Will you be sure to write me this year?"

"Let's all try to come back and be together again next year," Julie was saying. "And I'd like to vote Maggie the best camper in this bunk. . . ."

"Three cheers for Maggie," Carol took it up. "She's a jolly good fellow."

Maggie had a hard time falling asleep that night. But she had an even harder time saying good-bye the next morning. She certainly would miss the girls. Though they had promised to write and perhaps maybe

117

she could go visiting, she would miss waking up with them each morning and the busy life they had together here. Everyone was in city clothes again but this time Maggie saw them in a different way. Now these girls were her firm friends. They knew and understood each other. They all hated to part and with Abbey they went for a last walk around camp, saying good-bye sadly.

That evening when she got off the train at Pittsford there were no tears for Maggie. When she saw her mother and father this time she was radiating happiness and excitement. She didn't sound like the same girl who had seen them only three weeks before. She couldn't stop talking this time either, but now she was trying to get them to promise that she could go back to camp again next year.

"Gosh," she exclaimed as she ran up to her own room. "It will seem awful not to have my bunk mates tonight. Carol and Beth have to sleep on the train tonight. And here I am home already. Mom, do you think I could ask one of the girls—and if we could borrow a cot we could have two—here for Thanksgiving?"

"So you ended up by liking it?" Mom was saying.

"Liking it?" Maggie asked, sheer disbelief in her voice. "I loved it! Just as you said I would." Maggie ran to her mother and then her father, giving them each a big hug. "Thanks so much for letting me go. And the next rainy day, Mom, we can both sit and talk camp, and go over the pictures."